On the Edge of My Shadow

The Reincarnation of Michael Kenney

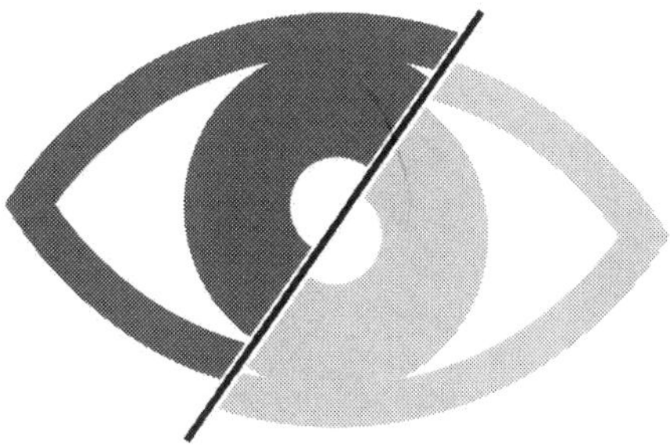

On the Edge of My Shadow

The Reincarnation of Michael Kenney

Kenneth M. Krakaur

Bujew Press

On the Edge of My Shadow
The Reincarnation of Michael Kenney

Published by Bujew Press

For further information, please contact:
Kenneth M. Krakaur at bujewpress@gmail.com.

Cover and book design by Tom Crockett
tomcrockett@mac.com

Printed in the United States of America

On the Edge of My Shadow
The Reincarnation of Michael Kenney
Kenneth M. Krakaur

1. Title 2. Author 3. Fiction

ISBN: 978-1468000221

Dedication

To my wife, Priscilla, who puts up with my sailing and writing obsessions.

To my children, Allison and Rachel, who have shared many days sailing on *Last Call* and *Instant Karma*.

To my grandson, Andrew, a future Chesapeake Bay sailor.

To those who have wondered about their lives—past, present and future.

Special Thanks

To Stuart Mark for his inspiration and technical guidance. You have been with me every step of the way.

To Kathleen Patrick, Fred Schriever, Jenny Jones, and Michael Maddocks, manuscript reviewers.

Preface

On the Edge of My Shadow

On the edge of my shadow is where you will find me,
Hiding and dreaming and wishing to be free,
Alive in the past, future, and present,
Wishing I could be you and you could be me.

On the edge of my shadow is where you will find me,
Once a live soul adrift on the sea,
Searching for answers to questions of my life,
Hoping to find the origin of me.

On the edge of my shadow is where you will find me,
Now with understanding of how life will be,
No longer concerned about my present awareness,
My soul has been given to you from me.

Stuart Mark

Chapter 1

Blink

Even with the smallest bit of light, there cast a shadow. Sometimes the shadows are so faint we ignore them. Even on bright sunlit days we rarely acknowledge our shadows. We seem to be bored with them or take them for granted. Rightly or wrongly we assume that our shadows are reflections of ourselves. But what if our shadows are not a reflection of ourselves but rather a reflection of our past or future?

Dr. Irving Blink was a well-known and well-respected physician in the Cape Town medical community. He was double board-certified in both pediatric medicine and child and adolescent psychiatry. At the marina, everyone called him D.B. but when I visited his office, I always addressed him as Dr. Blink. In his office, behind his desk was a picture of his father, Dr. Richard Blinkenstein. D.B. had shortened his name, dropping the "enstein" in order to disguise his Hebrew ancestry. He should have also dropped Irving in favor of a more Christian name. Dr. Blink was a tall man whose hair and eyebrows resembled Albert Einstein. He owned a Swan monohull named *Head Case*, a name properly chosen for a person who was clearly obsessive compulsive. Blink spent mòre time on boat maintenance than sailing, as evidenced by the pristine condition of his boat.

James and I had taken Ruby to my parents' house in Scarborough where she was spending a few days. This gave James and me some time away from the chore of raising a five-year-old, but more importantly, allowed for the needed time to follow up with Dr. Blink.

D.B.'s office was in a medical office building next to Cape Town Medical Center where my father had once worked. His office was plain and very organized. We arrived at the office an hour before his first appointment as we needed a fair amount of time to consult with the doctor. He escorted us back to the conference room which was as tidy as his boat.

"James, Jade, come in and have a seat."

"Thanks, Dr. Blink."

On the conference table were six folders. Each folder was perfectly positioned on the table, equidistant from each other. There were labels on each folder, also perfectly aligned. You could really see his obsessive compulsive behavior in action. He sat across from us, folded his hands and began to talk.

"Well, the six tests that Ruby took were unremarkable. Her IQ stats show that she is above average. She shows no signs of autism or other mental or behavioral abnormalities. Her blood work was normal. She appears to be very curious and quite intuitive for a five-year-old. I think what you have here is a child with an overactive imagination. I was very impressed with all that she told me during our testing sessions. Do you know where she is getting all this information and detail?"

"No, all of these imaginary friends started to show up about twelve months ago. She spends hours talking to them as if they are in the room. It's so strange. Lately she has started to talk to her shadow as if the shadow is one of these invisible friends. By the way, do you have any insight as to why she is so fascinated by fans?"

"I asked her that question during the testing and her reply was simply 'FLASH.' I asked her what FLASH meant and she said that it was one of the places where her friends live. I decided not to question her about that as I didn't want her to clam up."

There was a long pause in the conversation until Dr. Blink spoke up. "We could try hypnosis."

"No, I don't like that idea."

"Me neither," James said.

"Well then, let's just give it time and see if things settle down. If you want to move to hypnosis you can consider that at a later date. My advice is to stop worrying. She will be fine."

"Thanks, Dr. Blink. Oh, I have one more question. Of all your patients, how many have eyes like Ruby's?"

"Do you mean one blue eye and one brown eye?"

"Yes, exactly."

"Of all my patients, she is the only one. Has it shown up in any other members of your family?"

"No, not in my family but it has shown up in a friend of mine who died some years ago. And just in case you wanted to ask, that person is not Ruby's father, at least not in the biological sense."

"Well, if not the biological sense, then in what sense?"

"That, Dr. Blink, we will hold for another day." He said nothing.

For the next forty-five minutes we hashed and re-hashed the results. Dr. Blink was acting a little more cautious with his answers than I had noticed before. Then the conversation came to an abrupt end. "Will I see you at the marina over the weekend?" I asked.

"Yes, I'll be down there."

"Are you planning to go out for a sail?"

"No, I have some maintenance to do."

"No surprise there," I thought to myself. Then he escorted us to the door and we left, feeling somewhat conflicted.

"So Jade, what do you think?"

"I think he knows more than he is letting on."

"Why do you feel that way?"

"Blink is a detail junkie. His diagnosis was way too simple and abbreviated. He knows more than he is telling us."

"How do you know?"

"Ruby told me all the things that Blink had asked her, and she told me how she answered all of the questions. I'm telling you, Blink has a diagnosis but is afraid to disclose it. Don't you see, he is afraid of being wrong."

"What do you think Ruby's issue is?"

"I'm not sure but I don't think it is psychological. I think it is spiritual. I think she has a spiritual sense about herself that invites others in. And I don't think these imaginary friends are really imaginary. Have you listened to the conversations she has with these friends? There is no way she could have this level of insight into the dialogue. Someone or something is talking to her or she is repeating things she is hearing. I'm telling you, she is reaching back into the past. I really think she is Michael or at least some affiliated spirit of him."

"Jade, come on, you can't be serious."

"James, trust me on this one. You never met Michael Kenney. I have. I can feel his presence at times and I feel it through Ruby."

Chapter 2

Shadows

The drive to Scarborough seemed to take a very long time. James and I spent most of the drive rehashing the hour we spent with Dr. Blink. James was convinced I was overreacting to D.B.'s findings but I knew otherwise, so we went to quiet mode until we arrived at my parents' home. My mother met us at the door signaling us to be quiet.

"What's going on?" I asked.

"You need to see this. Then you can tell me what's going on with Ruby."

We walked to the back of the house to the guest room and peered in through the crack in the door. Ruby was sitting on the floor, facing the pale yellow painted wall. She had taken the three table lamps off the night stands and dresser and had placed them on the floor. Each lamp was turned on, which created three distinct shadows on the wall. Ruby sat there in a trance for several seconds and then slowly turned to the far-right shadow and started to talk.

"How are things going on the ice cream farm?" Ruby sat there waiting for a reply. "Did anyone get hurt in the fire?" She turned to the other shadows. "Isn't that terrible what happened to them on the farm?" She looked back at the first shadow. "Where is the farm? Where is Virginia?" I looked at James in disbelief. We backed away from the door and quietly walked to the living room.

"Okay, James, you heard it. How can you explain that?"

"I don't know how she knows about Virginia. Maybe we should ask her."

"That's exactly what I'm going to do." We walked back to the guest room and walked in. Ruby was startled by our appearance.

"Mommy, Daddy!" Ruby jumped to her feet and hugged both of us.

"So Ruby, what are you doing? Why are the lamps on the floor and who were you talking to?"

"I was talking to my friends."

"Tell me about your friends."

"My best friend is a girl who lives on a farm where ice cream grows. There are a lot of Bushmen that work on the farm. My friend is a Bushmen."

"Ruby, what is her name and where does she live?"

"Her name is Angel and she lives in Virginia."

"Where is Virginia?"

"I don't know. Let me ask her. Angel, where is Virginia?" There was a long pause as Ruby sat staring at the shadow on the wall. "Angel says that Virginia is in Merica."

Then James spoke up. "Ruby, who are your other friends?"

"I don't know their names, I just met them today."

"Why don't you say goodbye to your friends for now. Grandma is going to make lunch."

"Okay. Goodbye Angel. Goodbye new friends."

I reached down and turned off the lamps. "So James, do you believe me now or am I overreacting?"

Lunch was served on the patio. Ruby sat in her favorite chair which looked out into the backyard. Her shadow appeared intermittently as the sun repeatedly ducked behind the passing clouds. She repositioned herself in her chair so she could see her shadow more clearly. She sat there staring, as if she was waiting for the shadow to move independently from herself. Mom set the grilled cheese sandwiches on the table, sliding one in front of Ruby. Ruby picked up the sandwich, took a bite and then extended her arm and hand toward the shadow.

"Angel, do you want a bite? Are you hungry? Have you had lunch yet?"

Her hand stayed extended until a cloud took away the shadow. She relaxed her arm and took another bite of the grilled cheese sandwich. Then the sun reappeared and so did the shadow.

"If you get hungry later, Grandma will make you some cookies, right, Grandma?"

My mother looked over at me, not knowing how to answer the questions. "Ruby, maybe Angel's mother should make her some food," I suggested.

"She can't. Her mother is too busy picking ice cream."

"Tell me more about the ice cream, Ruby."

"Well, the ice cream is white and it grows on brown branches."

"Does it ever melt?"

"No. It's always the same, it never melts."

"James, bring the laptop computer in here. I want to see if we can identify the ice cream plant." James returned with the laptop, launched the search engine and typed in ice cream plant. There were no hits. "James, try cotton plant." A few seconds later, a picture of the cotton plant appeared. I turned the screen toward Ruby. "Is this the ice cream plant?"

"Yes, that's it."

"When Angel picks the ice cream plants do they use any farm equipment?"

"No, they use horses and wagons."

"Ruby, how old is Angel?"

"I don't know, maybe five like me. I think her brother is older."

"Have you ever talked to her brother?"

Ruby didn't answer. She simply stared back at the shadow. Then she started to talk again.

"Angel says I can't talk to you anymore about her or her brother."

Then she turned in her chair and looked toward the backyard. James shot a mysterious glance my way and raised his eyebrows. Then silence fell over the room.

Chapter 3

The Bundle

It had been a week since the bizarre events that had taken place at my parents' house. Ruby had stopped talking to her shadows and thoughts of our discussion with Dr. Blink had been set aside. Things for the most part seemed normal, however, that was about to change.

Sara Bellim was a clinical nurse specialist who worked for Dr. Blink. She and her husband rented a slip at the marina for their twenty-seven-foot sloop. Sara had many attributes of insignificance, especially for someone who was well educated. Her major flaw, however, was her flapping jaw. Her sense of patient confidentiality was non-existent.

"So Jade, how is the little genius?" asked Sara as she approached the counter at the marina office.

"Hello Sara, and what do you mean by that comment?"

"Dr. Blink didn't tell you?"

"Tell me what?"

"That Ruby really maxed the genius test bundle."

"What's a test bundle?"

"It's a battery of tests that can determine if someone is a genius and whether they have predictive intuition."

"Explain predictive intuition. I'm not familiar with the term."

"Well, if someone has predictive intuition, then they can predict certain events before they occur or may be able to guess correctly 70 percent to 80 percent of the time."

"Are you talking about ESP?"

"Generally that's the idea."

"Sara, can people who possess this ability see things that have happened in the past even if they have no knowledge about such events?"

"Maybe, but I will tell you this; Ruby's scores were the highest I have ever seen. In the test where you show someone a blank piece of paper and ask them to tell you what is drawn on the other side, Ruby scored in the 90th percentile. Dr. Blink was amazed at those results. Ruby is not an ordinary child. The kid is a solid genius. But you probably knew that already. Parents are normally really tuned into this type of behavior."

"Oh sure, James and I knew it all along," I said in my most convincing voice. "So, what brings you into the office?"

"Two bags of ice and a few granola bars."

"Shall I put it on your account?"

"Sure."

Then Sara grabbed the sundries and walked out of

the office. Moments later I was on the cell phone calling James.

James answered the phone. “Hey Jade, what’s up?”

“I just had the strangest discussion with Sara Bellim. She told me about a test that Ruby had taken when she was at Dr. Blink’s office. I wonder why he never disclosed the results during our meeting.”

“What type of test was it?”

“Basically it was an ESP test. Sara said Ruby scored in the 90th percentile and that she was a genius. She also said that Ruby may be able to recall historical events even if she had no prior understanding of such events.”

“Did she say why Dr. Blink never mentioned anything about the test?”

“No, and I didn’t press her.”

Then there was a long pause in the discussion and I could tell that James had turned his attention to another problem. “James, what are you doing?”

“Sorry. Dr. Blink just showed up at the marina and has asked me to come aboard to look at his engine.”

“Well go do that. I am going to get Ruby and get some lunch.”

“Okay, I will catch up with you later on.”

Then James terminated the cell phone call, so I walked over to our private office where Ruby was sitting at the desk.

“Hi sweetheart, what are you doing?”

“I’m drawing pictures.”

“What are the pictures about?”

“We are at a funeral and there is the person who died.”

A chill came over me. "Who is the dead person?"

"Dr. Blinkenstein!"

"Do you mean Dr. Blink's father?"

"No, Irving Blinkenstein, my doctor."

"Ruby, how do you know this?"

"Mom, didn't you smell it when Dr. Blink walked past the office?"

"Smell what?"

"Death. Didn't you smell death when Dr. Blink walked by the office?"

"No Ruby, I don't know what death smells like. Tell me."

"Think of the sweetest smell you can, and then make it even sweeter and sweeter until you feel like you are going to throw up."

"How do you know that's the smell of death?"

"Because that is what I smell when my friends appear in my shadows or in the ceiling fans."

"Ruby, do you think I should tell Dr. Blink?"

"You can, if you want to."

"Ruby, stay right here. I'll be right back." I ran to the other office and picked up the cell phone. Then I started to run down the pier toward Dr. Blink's boat. My heart was pounding with anxiety. As I approached the boat, James came topside.

"Jade, there is something wrong with Blink. He collapsed down below and is non-responsive."

"I know. Ruby told me that Blink was going to die. I have already called for an ambulance. Come on, let's see if we can do CPR on him until they get here."

James and I started CPR hoping that the emergency medical personnel would arrive momentarily.

"James, go get Sara Bellim, quick!" James ran over to the next pier as I continued to work on Blink. Then I looked up to see Ruby, standing in the cockpit. "What are you doing here?"

"I have a new picture for you."

"Not now, Ruby." Then she threw the picture down the companionway. It floated down and landed next to Dr. Blink. It was a picture of him sitting up in a hospital bed. At that moment, two EMTs descended into the cabin and took over. I stood there watching as the EMTs shocked Blink back to life. Minutes later he was taken to the ambulance and rushed to Cape Town Medical Center.

As I started to climb the cabin stairs, I saw Ruby still standing in the cockpit.

"Mommy, don't worry, Dr. Blink will be okay."

Chapter 4

The Smell of Death

The flowers that Ruby carried were too large for her grip. I had tried to encourage her to let me carry them but she was not in the mood to give in and I was not in the mood to debate her. The hallways in the Cape Town Medical Center were familiar to me, as I remembered the days spent in the hospital following Ruby's birth.

Dr. Blink's semi-private room was at the end of the hallway. He shared it with another person who was admitted with congestive heart failure. The door to the room was half opened, so we knocked and walked in. Dr. Blink was lying in bed, unaware that we had entered the room. He was staring at the ceiling, looking detached and a bit spaced out.

"Dr. Blink, are you up for visitors?" I asked in a sheepish tone. Blink looked over at us, reached for his glasses and acknowledged our presence.

"Jade, Ruby, please come in. This is a nice surprise."

"How are you feeling, Dr. Blink?" Ruby asked.

"I am feeling much better now, thanks to your Mom. You know she saved my life."

Ruby said nothing. "Actually, it was not me that saved your life. It was Ruby." Dr. Blink looked puzzled.

"How did that happen?"

"Dr. Blink, you know how she did it. We need to stop playing games with each other."

"What do you mean by that?"

"Sara Bellim stopped by the marina office the day you had your heart attack. She told me about the test bundle. It looks like you were not completely honest with us the day we had our consult." Blink sighed. He looked like a child who had just been caught lying to his parents. He looked ashamed and embarrassed but not enough to offer an explanation.

"Look, Dr. Blink, given that you owe Ruby and me your life, I think repayment can come with a little honesty." Blink said nothing at first and then spoke.

"Okay, I owe you an explanation." He paused and took a deep breath. "The test results were off the charts. They make no sense. I never saw scores as high as Ruby's. I was convinced that the results were flawed. In all my years of practice I had never seen a child Ruby's age score as high. In fact, I never saw any child of any age score so high. I didn't want to tell you as I didn't want to create false expectations."

"Is that the real truth or are you still holding back?"

"No, that's the truth, but how about a little honesty

from you."

Suddenly, James walked in the room and greeted Dr. Blink. The discussion quickly moved to his boat engine and I was temporarily off the hook. After the engine chat ended, the room filled with silence.

"James, why don't you take Ruby down to the gardens and show her the pretty flowers? I need to have a few minutes alone with Dr. Blink."

"Sure. Come on Ruby, let's go."

"So Dr. Blink, what do you want to know?"

"I want to know how Ruby knew I was having a heart attack and I'm curious about your friend who has eyes like Ruby's, the friend who you said is not her father."

"Okay, let me start with the heart attack. One of Ruby's imaginary friends is a girl named Angel. As far as I can tell, she not only sees the girl when she looks at her shadow, she sees the girl's surroundings. James and I believe that this girl is an American slave from the 1800s. This Angel person lives on a cotton farm, maybe a plantation, and it seems that there may be a lot of killing that goes on there. Ruby says she smells death when she talks to Angel. She also said she smelled death when you walked by the marina office. Then she started to draw a picture of your funeral. I just happened to walk in on her as she was completing it. Then I called the emergency medical people because I believe that Ruby sees into the future. As James and I were performing CPR on you, Ruby appeared on the boat with another picture. This one showed you in a hospital bed. Ruby said that you would be okay. At that moment the EMTs arrived and took over."

Blink listened very carefully, never questioning the validity of the facts. He was taking an inventory of the details to see if my story would help to validate the results of the test bundle.

"How long has Ruby been experiencing these shadow friends?" Blink asked.

"It's really been over this last year. And by the way, these friends are also starting to show up when Ruby stares at spinning objects, like ceiling fans. I have watched her have conversations with these friends. It seems to occur when she lies on her back and looks up at the moving fan blades."

"Yes, she told me that her friends live in the fans. She used the word FLASH to describe that. The whole thing is very strange and very interesting. I think we should talk more about hypnosis in order to get to the bottom of this."

Before I could respond, Blink's nurse walked in and requested that I leave.

"Dr. Blink has a date with the radiology department. I need to transport him to the main floor immediately."

"Jade, come see me tomorrow. You have one more question to answer."

"I'll check my schedule. Feel better, Dr. Blink."

"Thanks and thanks again for the flowers."

When I arrived at the garden, James and Ruby were walking the meditation labyrinth. She was walking slowly, studying each brick that created the winding pathway. James recognized my presence but Ruby did not. I watched her for several minutes and was amazed by her concentration. Each step she took was defined and calculated. She appeared to be meditating or maybe she had put herself in a hypnotic state. Finally she woke from her trance and looked over to me.

"Ruby, was that fun?" I asked.

"Yes, Mommy. Daddy, Angel and I really liked it."

Chapter 5

Dreams of Michael

There is a fine line between good dreams and nightmares. Sometimes good dreams turn bad and sometimes nightmares turn out okay. Then there are recall dreams. These are the type of dreams that haunt you. They repeat and repeat, night after night. Each time you re-enter the same dream you try to get a deeper glimpse into the meaning. Even when you do, you find that you can't quite remember all the detail; somehow the details evaporate as you start the waking process.

It had been fifteen consecutive nights that I dreamt about Michael Kenney. It seemed strange to have started this dream sequence about a person I hadn't seen in ten years. Our time together totaled less than an hour, but in that time he had done two very important things for me. Unbeknownst to me, he placed me in his will. Sometime after his will was settled, I ended up with his ownership in Mac Delivery Service and Marina. Then there was his prediction about the birth of Ruby. And now Ruby had brought Michael back into my life, yet again.

The first part of the dream takes me back to the beginning when I had signed on with a delivery crew to deliver a South African-built catamaran from Cape Town to the British Virgin Islands. I had just told my parents about my decision to quit my assistant chef job in favor of a new life of adventure as a cook on the high seas.

It was my last night working on shore, and business at Smyth's Bistro was unusually slow, so I said my goodbyes and was out of the restaurant by 10:30 p.m. On my way back to my room I decided to stop by Reubens, one of the most upscale restaurants in Cape Town. I always wanted to go there but never had.

"One drink at the bar to celebrate my departure from Smyth's and then back on the road," I thought. That was the plan, clean and simple. Things just didn't turn out that way.

When I arrived at Reubens, the bar was empty. I took a seat near the middle and lit up a cigarette, expecting it to be the last. I ordered a martini, dry and dirty, and on the rocks. I was in an odd talkative mood so I scanned the bar for a friendly face. Down at one end of the bar was a man who looked to be close to forty years old, drinking what I had just ordered, and reading a sailing magazine. When my drink came, I picked it up and walked to where he was sitting and introduced myself.

"Excuse me. I noticed you are reading a sailing

magazine. Are you a sailor?" He swiveled his chair around in my direction and looked at me expecting to see someone older. He was tall, thin, and had a warm and honest smile. I looked into his eyes. One was blue and one was brown. I had never seen anyone like that before.

"Yes, I sail in the Chesapeake Bay."

"Where's that?" I asked.

"In the U.S., East Coast, near Washington, D.C." Then he extended his hand and said, "Michael Kenney."

"How do you do, Mr. Kenney."

"Call me Michael."

"Very well, Michael."

"And your name?"

"Jade."

"Jade, nice to meet you." He reminded me of what my father may have been like twenty years earlier before the years of work stress corrupted his physical well-being.

"So Jade, thinking of buying a boat?"

"No sir, but I'm about to crew on a Bluewater 46."

"Nice boat."

Then I went on to tell him the whole story surrounding my impending trip. He listened very attentively. We both had another drink and then I asked, "Well, do you have any advice for me, Michael?" He took out his billfold and withdrew a small plastic packet, matchbook size.

"Jade, I want you to have this. It is filled with colored sand. This sand was given to me by Paul Curry, a dear friend of mine, back in the States. This sand comes from a Buddhist mandala, a sand painting. It has spiritual significance. It speaks of life's impermanence. The Tibetan monks who created this mandala, did so as part of a prayer ritual. The mandala is beautiful, and the effort that goes into its creation is immense. Shortly after the mandala is completed, it is destroyed. This is done to illustrate life's impermanence and to recognize that death is a part of life. They believe in reincarnation, as I do. You must carry it with you for the rest of your life. The sand will guide you.

"Jade, there are thirteen things you must remember. I will assume that your Judeo-Christian upbringing gave you ten; the sand will guide you to two of them. I will give you one. The first ten are the Ten Commandments. Modernize them as you wish. Numbers eleven and twelve come from the sand. You are in search of a new beginning. You are in search of inner peace. Inner peace can only come from the convergence of wisdom and compassion. When you don't know what to do, place the sand in your hand and remember: be wise, make your decisions carefully, use logic, not emotion. Be compassionate, think about others, make sure you understand how your decisions will affect others, look for the best in others and seek to understand before you seek to be understood. And number thirteen, I call the Platinum Rule. Do onto others as they would want done to themselves. Do not presuppose you know what is right for someone else. Godspeed, Jade."

I glanced down into my drink. The drink was empty. I looked up to Michael. He was gone. He vanished like a ghost in a dream. The only difference was the sand packet that lay in my hand as evidence that my ghost was real.

That night I went to my room and logged on to the Internet. Michael could not have known that I was totally out of touch with religion. I searched the Ten Commandments. There were many revisions and interpretations. When all was said and done I had my thirteen principles.

1. I will find a belief in a god
2. He will be my only god
3. I will not use his name in vain
4. I will designate time for prayer
5. I will honor my parents
6. I will not harm anyone or anything
7. I will not commit adultery
8. I will not steal
9. I will not lie
10. I will not desire what is not mine
11. I will always make careful decisions
12. I will be compassionate and caring
13. I will treat others as they wish to be treated

My second encounter with Michael occurred on Shirley Heights overlooking English Harbour in Antigua. The ride up to Shirley Heights with my friends was not very dramatic. After a few miles of winding roads and several potholes, we arrived. I paid the four-dollar cover charge, stopped by the bar, picked up a complimentary beer, walked through a passage and then onto the hill. Then it happened. Like being hit with a wall of ice cold water on the hottest day of your life — something came over me. I was stunned, shocked, and felt a feeling so unfamiliar to me. "I am so happy to be me," I thought. "I don't ever want to be anyone else or do anything different. I want to be me and I want to be here."

Then a man bumped into me, knocking my elbow. "Excuse me," he mumbled. He brought me back from my trance.

"What just happened?" I wondered.

Rachel, a friend of mine, approached me. "Are you okay?"

"Couldn't be better," I replied.

We all stood chatting and looking out at the most beautiful view of English and Falmouth harbours. Montserrat was visible some forty miles away and I felt that if I closed my eyes and reached out I would be able to touch it.

"Hey, how about a picture?" Allison said.

"Great idea." I pulled out my digital camera and looked for a bystander to capture the moment. There in front of me was the same man who had awakened me out of my trance fifteen minutes earlier. "Excuse me. Would you mind snapping a quick picture of me and my friends?"

"Be glad to. Ready, big smiles." The picture was taken. "Stay there, let me take another. Got it."

"Thanks." Then he handed the camera back to me. I flipped the switch to preview, glanced at the two pictures and looked up. He was gone. I felt a sudden panic, a familiar panic. I spun around looking in all directions but the stranger was nowhere to be found. I jumped onto a nearby rock, gaining a foot or two in height and saw the man moving through the crowd. I moved with great alacrity but once again my shortness handicapped me. Then I saw him. I approached him and tapped him on the back. He turned around.

"Excuse me, I … " It wasn't him. I had the wrong man. I looked all over but he was gone. Then it hit me. The voice. I knew the voice. It was Michael. No, it couldn't be. I would have noticed the eyes. This guy had brown eyes or was he wearing sunglasses?

Then I felt a tap on my arm. "Jade, are you okay? You look like you have just seen a ghost," said Allison.

"I may have." Then Yon, another friend, handed me another beer and the party resumed.

Later that night I ended up at Nick's Café. The partying that began on the mountain continued well into the morning. After many beers, many games of pool and a few sorry attempts at karaoke, I left Nick's and staggered back to the boat. The next morning I awoke with one of the worst hangovers of my life. I desperately needed a cup of black coffee and decided I was capable of making it. The first sip nearly burnt my lips so I added some cold water and continued to drink. Then I reached into my pocket. Something was wrong. Something was different. I retracted my hand. Lying in my palm was not one packet of sand, but rather, two packets. I had seen a ghost. I turned my head toward the sink and started heaving. What happened to me on Shirley Heights?

The following day I was given a letter that was left for me at the marina office.

Dear Jade,

Once again we meet for only a brief moment, before some event calls us to different directions. We obviously didn't recognize each other when I took your picture the other day. You look quite dif-

ferent.

Things have become very complicated for me. I would have liked to stay in Antigua but my boat was leaving early in the morning and I needed to start my journey back home. You see, life comes at you quickly. Sometimes you can dodge a bullet and sometimes you can't. All I can tell you is that I believe we will meet again. Where and when, I don't know, but time is of the essence. While my future is clear, yours is not. There are many things I wish to share with you but that will have to wait until our next meeting.

By the way, I slipped the sand into your pocket at Nick's last night, when you were shooting pool. I didn't want to break your concentration.

I trust that the thirteen principles have treated you well. How is the Bujew? If you ever get to Hampton Roads, Virginia, look me up, and if not, have a wonderful life.

Michael Kenney

The dream sequence ends with our third encounter. James and I were crewing on *Sur Le Vent* when the boat experienced mechanical problems. The owner decided to take her to a boatyard in Norfolk, Virginia. When the news spread of our change, I went to the communication room and logged onto the computer. I searched the web for Norfolk. I was linked to HR.com. HR was the abbreviation for Hampton Roads. I retrieved the letter from Michael and read the last line.

If you ever get to Hampton Roads, Virginia,

look me up, and if not, have a wonderful life.

"I can't believe this. I'm going to find him if it kills me," I said aloud.

Two weeks later we limped into Norfolk, Virginia, sailed down the Elizabeth River and turned over our ship to Sun Engineering. *Sur Le Vent* would be out of commission for thirty days. We were allowed to stay aboard during the time repairs were made. My galley duty was off the simple menu, so I had a lot of time on my hands. The second day of our stay it rained, so I spent most of my time on the Internet looking for Michael. All the name searches failed. Bujew failed. Then I had a hit. The search for "mandala" and "Hampton Roads" linked me to a newspaper article about Tibetan monks creating a mandala sand painting in Hampton, Virginia. I MapQuested the location. The monks would be in town next week. My luck was improving and I began to feel as if I was going to confront my ghost.

The next five days clicked by. James and the engineering staff worked alongside the repair crew from Sun. Tommy and Liz, the boat owners, were gone most of the time. My assistant was handling the galley and I was renting a car for the short drive to Hampton.

At 4 p.m. I arrived at the small auditorium in the village of Phoebus, part of the city of Hampton. I was so nervous. I expected to walk in and see Michael standing there, waiting for me, unable to vanish. I could hear the monks chanting. I could smell incense burning. The scent was delightful. My skin was full of goose bumps. There were thirty or so people milling around, looking at the monks work their magic with the sacred sand. The colors were vibrant, almost shocking. I approached the monks and watched them work and pray. I saw the very origin of my sand emerge. Then it hit me. Michael said it came from a friend named Curry. I left the monks and walked back to the lobby.

There was a man, fifties in age, wearing beads on his wrists and neck and talking to two monks. Our eyes met and locked on each other. He approached me. "Excuse me, I'm looking for Michael Kenney or a person named Curry. Do you know either of them?" He stared deep into my eyes, almost creating panic within me.

"I'm Paul Curry. You must be Jade." My knees started to feel weak. "I suppose you are here to see Michael."

"Yes, do you know where he is?"

"Yes, I see him every day. I will take you to him, but first I must get something from my office. Stay right here." He walked up a flight of stairs. I waited anxiously, wondering what he was doing. Then he walked down and signaled me to follow him. We walked out a side door, down an alley and onto the street.

"He is just around the corner. So, how has the sand treated you, Jade of South Africa?" I looked up at him. He was very tall. "Here we are," his mood changing to sadness.

"Where, he lives in a church?"

"No, he lives over there." Paul's arm was extended, his fingers pointing specifically to a large stone in the church's cemetery. "This is Michael Kenney's new home. He died two weeks ago." I started to collapse. Paul's large hand grabbed me under my arm to steady me. Tears poured down my face. I felt as empty as I ever felt in my life. I was lifeless. A part of me was dying.

"Jade." The voice startled me. "Walk with me." We walked, my knees shaking. We stopped in front of the stone. It read Michael Kenney. There was no birth date or death date. The stone looked to be hundreds of years old as if it had been used before, by others who had died and been buried at this church. I tried to make out other names but the engravings had been filled in with mortar. I wondered if Michael had been buried here before.

Then Paul helped me down to my knees. The sun on my face felt warm. All the noise around me had stopped except for the sound of birds nesting in a near-by tree.

His hand touched my shoulder. I looked up. "This is for you." He handed me a letter, one page folded in thirds and sealed by a single staple. "I have been holding this for you. Michael knew you'd be coming someday. He told me he didn't know when but he was sure that you would be coming." Paul walked away. I sat there crying as anyone would, who had lost a very close friend. I opened the letter. It was hard to read through my tears.

Dear Jade,

So we missed each other this time. My loss.

The sand you have carried is a reminder of life's impermanence. The monks create a mandala in honor of life and prayer and shortly thereafter destroy it, to demonstrate life's fragility. We Buddhists do not fear death. Death is a part of life. We are all reincarnated over and over again. It's a circle, not too different from the circle you and I have created. I found you in Cape Town and now you have found me. Continue your dreams, and your adventure. Someday you will fall in love. You will have children and you will return to Cape Town.

Everything that has occurred in this life has been for the sole purpose of our final meeting. The day I met your father many years ago, and our two meetings, are all part of the much larger plan. While all of this may be very confusing to you, someday it will make perfect sense as we will learn to love each other in ways you cannot imagine. This is our destiny.

Have a wonderful life, Jade, of South Africa.

Sincerely,
Michael Kenney

I looked back at Curry. He nodded. I looked back at the stone and reached into my pocket. I took out one packet of sand and held it in my hand. "Goodbye, Michael. Thanks for all you have done." The package fell from my hand, the seal breaking. Then the sand separated from the packet and rained over his grave.

Each time after I wake from my dream, I walk to my dresser and take out the letters he gave to me. I read them yet again and wonder why he picked me to bear the child that carries his soul. In some ways I feel lucky and even blessed and in other ways I feel cursed. Somehow those words in the letters were a forecast of my life, a pathway that for better or worse had no ability to be altered. *Some day we will learn to love each other in ways you cannot imagine. This is our destiny.* I hear these words repeating in my head every morning when I walk into Ruby's room. Sometimes I want to say, "Good morning Michael, what trick will you have Ruby do today? Well, yesterday she spoke to her shadow and someone named Angel answered back, and the day before that she became entranced by a ceiling fan, and oh, by the way, now she sees the future. So what's next, world peace?"

James had finally begun to accept all of this, though his acceptance had been shaky at times. His view of the world was very black and white and not usually open to ideas of reincarnation and soul transfer. But as Ruby continued to perform he had become a bit fascinated with the whole thing. He thought I should tell Dr. Blink about Michael Kenney. He speculated that somehow it would help all of us to better understand Ruby. The bottom line, however, was that the only people who needed to understand Ruby were us, and "us" did not include Dr. Blink.

I had been having thoughts about going back to the U.S., and spending some time with Michael's friends and family, but I didn't know how to just disengage from my current life. I needed to test this with James.

Chapter 6

The Telephone

Ruby had grown very fond of the telephone. Unfortunately she wasn't interested in talking to friends or family, at least not the living family. More and more new friends and names started to appear. They appeared in her shadows and in the trances and now on an unplugged telephone. Ruby was now six years old and her list of imaginary friends all seemed to be linked. She never talked to anyone about them other than to James and me. She never mentioned them to her school friends or the kids in the neighborhood. It was as if she was leading two lives.

My anxiety about the whole thing peaked when a new name appeared. Ruby had a new friend who she referred to as DataTwo. According to Ruby, DataTwo was a friend of Angel, who was a friend of Ghost. Ghost was also a friend of Sunset. On the surface this should not have given me that much anxiety, except that DataTwo had a boat, and DataTwo sometimes visited Cape Town and DataTwo had beautiful sand, which he gave to people. I began to wonder if DataTwo was really Daddy Two or Daddy Too. Had Michael taken on some spiritual role within Ruby? Did he see himself as her soul father? All this was starting to make me so crazy that I decided to seek advice from a professional.

Dr. Blink was very happy to see me as he greeted me at his office.

"Sit down, Jade. Can I get you a cup of coffee?"

"No thanks. I had my fill of caffeine already."

"So Jade, how is the little fortune teller doing?"

"This is no time for humor, Dr. Blink."

"I wasn't trying to be funny," Blink replied.

"I think it's time we move to the next step. At one time you mentioned that we should try hypnosis. At first I was really against this, but so much has developed and I think we need to get into Ruby's head."

"Well, there are many paths we can take. We can go for straight hypnosis or we can augment the hypnosis with some mild sedative. And then there are those drugs that will induce hallucination."

"No. No drugs."

"Okay. What do you want to accomplish with the hypnosis?"

"I want to understand more about these friends she is seeing, especially DataTwo."

"Tell me about DataTwo."

"Do you remember when James and I were in your office to review the test results and I asked you if you had ever seen anyone with eyes like Ruby?"

"Yes, you told me that a friend of yours had eyes like Ruby's, but that he was not the father."

"All that is true, however, this friend also told me in a letter that Ruby would somehow be linked to him, as if she would share his soul."

Blink looked puzzled.

"Jade, start at the beginning, tell me everything about this person and don't leave out any details."

"This will take awhile."

"No problem. I have the time."

I started at the very beginning, going over all the details: the meeting in the bar in Cape Town, the sand, the Bujew, his disappearing at Reubens and his reappearance on Shirley Heights. I described the events at his gravesite and the two letters he had left for me. Then I dropped the bomb.

"Dr. Blink, he wrote in the letter that *we would learn to love each other in ways you cannot imagine. This is our destiny.* I think he was trying to tell me that he would be reborn into Ruby; that we would learn to love each other as mother and child. The whole thing is totally creepy." Blink sat there speechless.

"So, what you are telling me is that Ruby is the reincarnation of this friend?"

"Yes, his name was Michael Kenney. He is the same person who left the marina to James and me."

"How well did you know this guy?"

"As I told you before, we talked for five minutes in Reubens, one minute on Shirley Heights and then there were the two letters. That's it. I meet him, we talk, I meet him again and don't know it's him. Then he writes me two letters, tells me he will reappear as my child and then he makes me a beneficiary on his will, leaving Mac Delivery Service and Marina to me and James. The whole thing is so bizarre and weird, but at the same time I feel lucky and special."

"Okay, let's say the whole thing is true—what do you want to learn from Ruby?"

There was a long pause. "I want to talk to Michael. I want you to make her reach Michael. I want to know why he picked me. I want to know who all these other people are that Ruby sees. I want to know if she is going to die young like Michael did. And I want to know how to get my little girl back from him and back from this world she is living in."

By now I was crying in total frustration. Blink pulled two tissues from the box on his desk, handing one to me and using the other to wipe the sweat from his bald head.

"Jade, you better talk this over with James and then get back to me. I really need to digest this conversation. I think I need to do a little research at the University on reincarnation and develop a care plan for Ruby. Can you tell me anything else about Michael Kenney? Do you know why he was in Cape Town when you first met him?"

"Yes, I recall that he was in town to lecture at the University."

"Do you know what year that was?"

"Gosh, it had to be fifteen years ago, I would assume."

"Okay, that's a great start. Let me see what I can find out about this Michael fellow. I'll call you as soon as I find something. And Jade—try to relax and get some rest."

Chapter 7

The Answer

Renil Pash was a tall black African who was completing his administrative fellowship for his degree in healthcare administration. He was also a former research assistant at the medical center before taking on his current position at the medical center hospital. I always found his name to be odd and wondered if his parents were dyslectic and were playing a cruel name game with their son. Renil entered my office looking shy and obsequious.

"Dr. Blink, it's nice to see you again. It's been a long time."

"Yes, it has. How is your fellowship going?"

"I think it is going well. I am hoping to get an offer from the hospital to work in cardiology management."

"Let me know if there is anything I can do to help, like a letter of reference or a phone call to the hospital executive."

"So, Dr. Blink, why did you call me here?"

"I was wondering if you could do me a favor."

"Sure, what?"

"I need to find out some information about a visiting lecturer who spoke at the University about fifteen years ago. He was an American named Michael Kenney. He died about ten years ago. He was a Buddhist and lived in the U.S. near Washington. I believe he may have lived in Virginia on the East Coast."

"What do you want to know about him?"

"I want to know anything and everything that you can find out."

"May I ask why?"

"A patient of mine is being haunted by this guy."

"Haunted, as in ghost?"

"Not exactly. Anyway, see what is available in the archives. I would start with the Continuing Education Coordinator."

"Okay, I will try to get back to you in the next week."

Tray C. Tracye had been an employee of the University medical school division for twenty-plus years. She was a tenth-generation South African, whose family landed in Cape Town running from the British Navy. The Tracye family had given up piracy in favor of a more conventional and civilized life on land. But more important than her lineage was her twenty years of knowledge about continuing education at the University.

"How can I help you?" Tray C. Tracye asked as she

looked up from her computer.

"Ms. Tracye, my name is Renil Pash. I am an administrative fellow at the hospital. Dr. Blink sent me over here to see if you could help me find some information for him. He is trying to get anything you may have in your files about a man named Michael Kenney. Dr. Blink said he lectured at the University some years ago."

"Okay, let me check the old files."

Tray C. Tracye walked over to the filing cabinet and pulled out a stack of files.

"Here are the annual reports for the continuing education program for the last twenty years. Take a seat over there. You are free to thumb through them."

"Thanks, Ms. Tracye."

"No need to be so formal. Just call me Tray C."

Starting with the oldest file, Renil looked through each annual report. The reports, averaging 20 pages in length, were fairly detailed. He carefully read each page as if searching for the proverbial needle in the haystack. Then, there it was: Michael Kenney—Religious and Spiritual Convergence.

Tray C. Tracye looked over to where Renil was sitting. "Did you find something?"

"Yes, I found it right here. He spoke at the University back in the 1990s."

"Let me see that," Tray C. Tracye said as she walked over to Renil. She picked up the report and started to read it."I remember that guy; he traveled with a monk." She continued to read. "Yes, he shared the lecture with this monk, Geshe Jodii Ruakark. He was a Tibetan monk. See." She pointed to the summary and accompanying bios. "His temple was in Washington, D.C. I remember that lecture. I attended both sessions. That Michael Kenney chap was electrifying. You said he died?"

"That's right, Ms. Tracye. "

"I wonder if the monk is still around. May I use your computer?"

"Sure, help yourself."

Renil started to search the Internet and within five minutes had located the temple's website and contact information. He thanked Tray C. for her help and returned to his office at the medical center.

The next day Dr. Blink took a call from Renil.

"So, Renil, what did you find out?"

"This Michael Kenney guy lectured alongside a Buddhist monk named Geshe Jodii Ruakark. I have the website of the temple where he worked and the contact information."

"Great work; email it to me."

"I already have—check your email."

"Thanks, Renil. You have been a great help."

Dr. Blink immediately picked up the phone and dialed Tray C. Tracye."

"Tray C. Tracye, how can I help you?"

"Hi, Tray, Dr. Blink here. First, I want to thank you for helping Renil. I also have two other requests. First, send me any information you have on Michael Kenney from the annual report, and by any chance, do you have a transcript of the lecture that Michael Kenney delivered?"

"Yes and no. We have the audio tapes from all lectures but they are not transcribed. I could get that done for you but you will be charged for the process."

"No problem. Have it done and send it to me in a PDF file."

"Okay, Dr. Blink. I will scan the annual report and email it to you and I will get the audio tape transcribed. The transcription will take about two weeks."

"That will be fine and thanks again."

Chapter 8

You've Got Mail

A familiar sound rang out from the laptop computer indicating another email had been deposited in the mailbox of Mac Delivery Service. Glancing over, I noticed the somewhat unfamiliar address Iblink@tacoma.com. I wondered why Dr. Blink was e-mailing me as it was not the way we normally communicated. I opened it up and read it.

> *"Jade,*
>
> *I have made contact with a friend of Michael Kenney. He is living in Washington, D.C., and we plan to talk next week. Do you know anything about a Tibetan monk named Jodii Ruakark? He was a co-lecturer with Michael Kenney when Michael lectured at the University many years ago. Please get back to me as soon as possible."*

I sat down and pondered the question. The only

person I had met that was a friend of Michael Kenney's was Paul Curry, and I hadn't communicated with him since Ruby's birth. I emailed Dr. Blink.

> *"Thanks for keeping me in the loop but I don't know this Jodii person, but I do know that Michael was close to some monks that taught at the Art Center in Hampton, Virginia. Let me do some research and get back to you in a day or so. See you next week."*

I immediately launched the search engine and searched for Paul Curry. Within seconds I had pages of hits. The most current was an article announcing Paul Curry's retirement from the American Theatre. The article chronicled all of the career accomplishments of Paul Curry, including a few sentences about his interest in Buddhism and the monks that annually taught at the Arts Center. The final sentence left me cold as it indicated that he had moved back to his birthplace in the UK and planned to retire there with his family. I terminated the search and started a new search of the American Theatre. After locating the site, I hit the contact button for the theater and started to type.

> *"Hi, my name is Jade Morison. I'm an old friend of Michael Kenney and Paul Curry. Is it possible to get a forwarding email address for Paul Curry? Thanks in advance, Jade Morison."*

Within minutes a new email appeared. The address was Maria@Amtheatre.com. I opened it up and started to read.

"Jade, How's Ruby?" A nauseous feeling came over me but I kept reading. *"Paul's new email address is pcurrry@sussexnet.uk. I am sure he would like to hear*

from you. Stay well."

The tone of the email was very strange, as if this person named Maria was emailing an old friend. And how did she know about my daughter? It was so weird, but par for the course considering Ruby's latest antics. I started typing an email to Paul when I was interrupted by a phone call. I recognized the number. It was a call from my mother.

"Hi, Mom."

"Hello, Jade. How's things at the marina?"

"Everything is fine. How's Ruby?" I asked.

"Good, I just picked her up from school and she is playing in the backyard. I was wondering if you said anything to her about her being hypnotized."

"No, I hadn't, and I'm sure James didn't either. Why are you asking?"

"I was watching her play on the swings and she was singing a song that she had obviously made up. I swore I heard her say, 'Here I swing on the tree, there'll be no hypnosis from Blink to me.' "

"Where is this weird stuff coming from," I said in a frustrated tone. "I wonder what other strange things are going to happen."

"I was wondering that myself."

"Anyway, thanks for calling and I'll be home around six."

"Okay, see you then."

I went back to the laptop and started to type.

"Dear Paul.

I hope this email finds you well. Congratulations on your retirement and return to the UK.

Maria from your office was kind enough to give me your email address. I am doing some research on Michael Kenney and am trying to find out information about an old friend of his named Jodii Ruakark. Do you know him and if so, can you tell me about him? I found out that Michael Kenney had lectured with him many years ago. You see, I am having issues with Ruby. She is six now and has developed all these imaginary friends. I think one may be Michael. I know this sounds somewhat weird but sometimes I think he is talking to her. She seems to know things about him which supports my feelings. Ruby's pediatrician is suggesting we hypnotize Ruby and see if she is really in contact with Michael.

I know all of this sounds bizarre but I really need your help. Thanks in advance. Jade "

I hit the send button and shut down the laptop. Then I walked out to the end of the dock where James was working and filled him in on all that had occurred over the last hour. James confirmed that he had not mentioned the "H" word to anyone and that he was beginning to have some reservations about the whole hypnosis idea.

An hour later we were home and sitting down to dinner. My parents had joined us and the dinner discussion was light until my father wandered into dangerous territory.

"So Ruby, did you speak to any of your friends today?"

"Yes Poppy, I talked to DataTwo."

"Oh really, and what did he say?"

"He said it was okay for Dr. Blink to talk to Jodii." The fork dropped from my hand and in the process of recovering, I knocked over a glass of water. The glass cracked and the water ran across the table, spilling onto Ruby's lap. She didn't move. She just kept eating. James returned with a towel and began soaking up water. I just sat there thinking to myself, "Why is he doing this to her and when is it going to stop?"

Chapter 9

The Journal

Two days had drifted by without a return email from Paul Curry and without Ruby mentioning anything about her imaginary friends. The reprieve was welcome from Ruby's standpoint but not from Paul Curry's. On the morning of the third day, things began to change. First was a short email from Maria at the theater. The e-mail simply said:

> *"Expect an e-mail from Paul any day. He is traveling back from India and should be back in Sussex today."*

There was no greeting or salutation in the email. I replied back.

"Thanks for the head- up."

Then the phone rang. Caller ID indicated "Unknown Caller." I answered the phone.

"Mac Delivery Service."

"Jade?"

"Yes, this is she."

"Paul Curry here."

A butterfly flew across my stomach. "Paul, how are you? I heard you've been traveling."

"Yes, I just got back from India."

"What's up in India?"

"I went over with a friend to do some meditation training."

"Really? Was the friend Jodii?"

"Yes. How did you know?"

"Lucky guess."

"So Jade, Michael's running havoc over you and Ruby."

"Yes, Paul. Somehow he appears to be able to speak to Ruby. Ruby has all these imaginary friends."

"How many?"

"Maybe six or seven."

"Any named Angel or Jost?"

"Yes, how did you know that?"

"Jade, just prior to Michael's death, he gave me a very extensive journal, a kind of autobiography of his life. I think you should read it. I can send you an electronic copy."

"What does it say?"

"The long and short is that Michael had made two important discoveries in his life and Ruby is an important part of the latter discovery. You see, somehow Michael could see images of his past and future. More specifically, he discovered where his soul had resided prior to the soul becoming his. And he also discovered where his soul would be going after his death. Michael described it as a preincarnation and reincarnation. Angel and Jost were his pre-incarnates. Angel's soul was passed to Jost, then Jost passed to Michael, and then Michael to Ruby. It's all in the journal, every detail."

"Why didn't you tell me about this before?"

"Michael told me only to share it with his family and I guess you now qualify. Does Ruby stare at ceiling fans?"

"Yes."

"Does she stare at the TV on blind channels?"

"No, but she does talk to her shadows. Did Michael do that?"

"No. Has Ruby said anything about Audrey or Su?"

"No. Who are they?"

"Audrey is Michael's wife and Su is his biological daughter."

"I didn't know he was married nor had a child."

"Su was born a few months after his death. She is eleven years old now."

"Paul, I need to see the journal."

"Okay, I'll email it to you tomorrow."

"May I share it with others?"

"Let's keep it close for now."

"Okay, it won't go beyond James and Blink."

"What's blink?"

"Dr. Blink is Ruby's pediatrician, the one who is suggesting that we hypnotize Ruby."

"The doctor's name is Dr. Blink? That's coincidental. Michael's journal is titled 'In the Blink of an Eye.'"

"That is strange. Tell me more about Audrey and Su."

"Not now. Let's hold that for another day after

you've read the journal."

"Okay, so what about Dr. Blink? Can I share it with him?"

"I guess you can, but let me warn you, you're in for a real roller coaster ride."

"I'm not surprised."

"Look, I'll call you in a few weeks after I read the journal."

"It was great talking to you, Jade."

"Same here, Paul, and thanks for everything. By the way, Dr. Blink is scheduled to talk to Jodii Ruakark in the next few days."

"That will be very interesting."

"Why?"

"I think Jodii will be able to shed some light on what's going on with Ruby and Michael."

"Well, I guess we will see. Paul, take care."

"You, too."

The following day the expected email arrived. The only thing in the email was an attachment. I opened the PDF file. It was 350 pages. I decided not to read even the first sentence and instead sent it to the printer. Ten minutes later, two copies of the journal were printed. I took them down to an office supply store and had both copies spiral-bound. Then I called James. He answered the phone in his typical British style.

"Hello, love."

"It's here."

"What's that?"

"Michael's journal."

"Great. Are you still up for our getaway?"

"Sure, I'll let Mom know."

James and I had decided that when the journal arrived we would go away for a few days and relax in the wine country. We booked a reservation at a nice bed and breakfast in Franschhoek. Our getaway agenda was simple: wine, food, love, and reading. Maybe we would finally begin to understand what was happening to our daughter.

Chapter 10

The Reading

The B&B had a magnificent view of the surrounding mountain ranges and was the perfect setting for accomplishing the task at hand. The first day, the weather was delightful so we put the journal aside and wine-hopped through the vineyards. I remembered so well the feeling of falling in love with James and was so glad we had each other during these strange times. On day two of the getaway the clouds and the rain moved in so we dealt with the other two agenda items. By late morning we were ready to get into the journal. We decided to read it aloud to each other, switching readers every twenty to thirty pages.

Page after page we learned about the sad and twisted life of Ruby's pre-incarnate. The stories of Angel Lehcar, Jost and Sonnet were mesmerizing. The journal got particularly odd when, first my father, then I appeared in the text. It was so illuminating and yet terrifying to see how Michael viewed me and our encounters, and how I became a part of his plan and his future. We learned about his addiction to the spinning fans and how he would lie on his bed staring upward, blinking his eyes to the rhythm of the turning fan blades until the images appeared. The images he saw were a glimpse into the past and the future and became the reason for his existence and his never ending need to understand where his soul had been and where it would eventually go.

And then there was Audrey, the woman he truly loved but never pursued, somehow lost to the present. Yet from speaking to Paul, I guessed he eventually connected with Audrey at the very end. And that between Audrey and me, and knowing where his soul would go after his death, he became complete.

There was one concern, however, and that was the cause of his death. Both he and his pre-incarnate, Jost, appeared to have died from a brain tumor. It made me wonder what would happen to Ruby.

After reading the journal we were filled with every emotion possible, but fear and exhaustion were the most prevalent. That night neither one of us was able to sleep. We stayed up hashing and rehashing all of the details in the journal. I felt the need to run home and hug Ruby and rush her off to the hospital and have her checked for a brain tumor. I wanted to get on an airplane and fly to Virginia and visit Audrey. I wanted to meet Michael's daughter Su and for them to meet Michael's other daughter; his reincarnate. I wanted to have Ruby talk to Audrey as a medium between Michael and her, and for Michael to see the daughter that was born just after his death. But Ruby was not a vehicle for our reconnecting Michael and his past life; she was my daughter and I needed to protect her from the invasion of Michael Kenney.

I was beyond conflicted, with a storm of internal emotions and no clear sense of right and wrong. All I knew was that I wanted to go home, back to Cape Town. I wanted to hold Ruby in my arms, to care for her and to love her. And then there was Dr. Blink and the hypnosis. Should we go forward with it or should we not? James did a lot of listening and then rendered his opinion.

"Jade, for every question there are many answers. We will never know what is right and what is wrong. I believe we should not give Dr. Blink a copy of the journal, but I think we should go forward with the hypnosis."

"Why do you feel this way?"

"I think we need to discover what Michael wants and if we understand that, then maybe we can get him to go on his way. I also think we need to keep Blink in a box. We need to have a superior understanding about Michael Kenney and Ruby. Maybe after the hypnosis we can let him read his journal."

"What about our parents?"

"We keep the journal between you and me for now. Maybe after the hypnosis we will let them read it. Can you live with those decisions?"

"I think so. Let's talk about it some more on the ride home."

"Okay."

Five minutes into the ride home I was sound asleep and dreaming. I was back at Reubens during our first encounter. Each second of our brief meeting was replayed in detail. Then I was on the mountaintop at Shirley Heights and once again, each moment of the encounter was replayed. Next I was on my knees at Michael's gravesite, crying and wondering about the letter and what it really meant. The dreaming continued. Ruby was swinging on her tree swing. She turned and looked at me and her face was Michael Kenney's. Then she turned back and looked at me again. This time it was an older girl. She was pretty and she smiled at me. I smiled back and called her Su. Then I walked outside and looked over to the neighbor's yard. There was a strange woman standing there. She was tall and slender and very beautiful. She called out to me, "Jade, Jade." I called to her. "Audrey, Audrey." Then I looked up and felt a hand on my shoulder. "Jade, wake up." It was James's voice but I couldn't open my eyes. I couldn't wake up. There was an Asian man beside me. "Jodii, is that you?" but before he could answer, the voice interfered.

"Jade we're home, wake up."

This time my eyes opened. It was dark outside and I could see our house. Ruby was standing by the window. My heart moved to her and away from the dreams.

Chapter 11

The Hypnotic Equation

Three days later I got a phone call from Dr. Blink. He told me that he had a copy of Michael Kenney's lecture, that he had read it, enjoyed it immensely, and that he was ready to start the hypnosis if we were still interested. I told him that we were and set up an appointment for the first session. Ruby had not said anything about the hypnosis since she sang about it ten days earlier.

As we approached the entrance to Blink's office, Ruby spoke up.

"Mommy?"

"Yes, Ruby."

"DataTwo said hypnosis is okay."

"Really? When did he say that?"

"While you and Daddy were driving." James and I said nothing.

Once again Dr. Blink's office was empty. He greeted us at the door and patted Ruby on the head.

"How are you doing, Ruby?"

"Fine, Dr. Blink. How are you?"

"Fine."

"You'll be okay, Dr. Blink. You are not going to die today."

"Ruby, please be respectful. You owe Dr. Blink an apology."

"Sorry, Dr. Blink."

"It's all right, no need to apologize."

We continued down the hall to a small conference room. The room had four leather chairs in it, each one looking very comfortable.

"Have a seat," Blink announced.

We each took a seat and then sat for a moment in silence. There was a folder on a small table that sat by the chair occupied by Dr. Blink. It was labeled "Kenney Lecture." Blink repositioned himself in the chair and began to speak.

"Ruby, how do you feel? Are you relaxed?"

"Sort of."

"What would make you more relaxed?"

"May I take off my shoes?"

"Sure."

"Ruby, is there anything else that would make you more relaxed?"

"No."

"Are you tired?"

"A little bit."

"What makes you happy?"

"Swinging on my tree swing."

"Okay then, close your eyes and make believe that

you are swinging." Ruby closed her eyes and said nothing.

"Can you feel the nice breeze on your face?"

"Yes."

"Can you hear anything other than my voice?"

"No."

"Good. Keep swinging." Ruby said nothing.

"Ruby, who is DataTwo?"

"Michael."

"Is Michael your friend?"

"Yes."

"Do you know his other name?"

"Kenney." James and I shot each other a glance.

"Can you talk to your friend now?"

"Yes."

"Okay, just keep swinging." Dr. Blink opened the folder.

"Ruby, can you speak to DataTwo?"

"Yes."

"Good. Where did DataTwo lecture when he was in Cape Town?" Ruby suddenly opened her eyes and stared at Blink. Dr. Blink looked momentarily uncomfortable.

"I lectured at the University." Now we all looked at each other.

"Ruby, why did you say 'I'?"

"I am DataTwo." I started to say "Stop this" but James grabbed my arm, indicating his approval to continue.

"DataTwo, who lectured with you?"

"Jodii."

"Do you remember your speech?"

"Yes."

"Can you recite any of the speech?"

"Good afternoon, ladies and gentlemen. I am delighted to be here at this prestigious University to talk to you about one of my most favorite topics." Ruby paused.

"Thank you, DataTwo. That was very good, and word-for-word from your remarks." Then Ruby started to speak again.

"Third paragraph begins, I am a Bujew… fourth paragraph begins, Religious convergence is necessary…" Blink's expression indicated 100 percent accuracy. Ruby closed her eyes. Everyone took a deep breath.

"Michael. May I call you that?"

"Yes."

"Tell me about Ruby's friends." Ruby's eyes opened.

"I am Michael. I am Angel. I am Jost. I am Ruby." Ruby's eyes closed.

"Michael, is there something you want or something we can do for you?" Tears began to roll down Ruby's cheeks. "What is it, Michael? Please tell me." Ruby said nothing. "Ruby, where is Michael?"

"DataTwo is gone."

"Where did he go?"

"I don't know. He just left."

"Are you ready to get off the swing?"

"Yes."

"Okay Ruby, when I snap my fingers, the swing will stop and you will be awake. Okay, Ruby?"

"Yes."

Then Dr. Blink leaned toward Ruby, placing his

hand by her ear and snapped his fingers. Ruby opened her eyes as if she was waking up from a long sleep.

"How do you feel, Ruby?"

"Fine."

"What was the last thing you remember?"

"I had just taken off my shoes and you were saying something about my tree swing." Then Ruby looked over at me. "Mommy, can we get some ice cream?"

"Sure, whatever you want."

"Well Jade, I'll follow up with you tomorrow."

"Great. Thanks, Dr. Blink." As I stood up, I could feel a chill roll down my back.

Chapter 12

Connecting the Dots

Ever since James and I read Michael's journal, I was bothered by the idea of Dr. Blink talking to Jodii. My insight into the relationship between Michael and Jodii was now more in-depth as Jodii was written about extensively within the pages of the journal. In some way I felt Jodii was mine and I didn't want Dr. Blink speaking to him without me there to hear what was said. I was determined to interfere with any discussion between the two of them. I phoned Dr. Blink. His receptionist answered and immediately got him on the line.

"Hello, Jade."

"Hi, Dr. Blink."

"What can I do for you today?" Dr. Blink asked.

"Dr. Blink, I have a question and possibly a request of you."

"Okay. What is the question?"

"Have you talked to Jodii yet?"

"No. We have traded phone calls all week but I have not connected with him."

"Well then, Dr. Blink, I have a request."

"What's that?" Blink asked.

"I don't want you to talk to him until I say it's okay."

"Why?"

I searched for an answer that would not expose the fact that I had a copy of Michael's journal. "It's complicated. But let me be more frank. If you talk to Jodii it will hamper our ability to continue Ruby's therapy."

"Why? I feel like you're holding me hostage," Blink said defensively.

"I am holding you hostage but I also think you need to comply with the wishes of your client and patient. Do we have a deal, Dr. Blink?"

"I suppose so, but I must tell you I don't like it a bit."

"I'm sorry, but it has to be this way."

"Fine. So when do you want to come in for the next session?"

"I don't know but most likely in a few weeks. By then I will have a better understanding of where our questioning should go."

"And will that come from Jodii?"

"Very possibly."

"Okay Jade, the ball is in your court."

"Very good, Dr. Blink." I hung up without saying goodbye. Seconds later the phone rang. It was Blink.

"Jade, do you need Jodii's phone number?"

"Sure."

"Remember there is a six-hour time difference."

"Thanks, Dr. Blink."

At 4 p.m. I dialed the number that Blink had provided. The call was answered by a person saying the name of the temple but due to his accent, I could not decipher the name.

"Hello, I'm looking for a Geshi Jodii Ruakark."

"Sorry, Geshi Jodii is gone."

"Gone? Where did he go?"

"He is traveling to the monastery in Atlanta. He can be reached there later today."

"May I have the phone number there?"

"Yes." The person gave me the number and hung up as if he was in a rush.

It was now approaching midnight and I decided to call the monastery. The phone rang and was answered immediately.

"Drepung Loseling, how can I help you?"

"Hello. I'm trying to reach Geshi Jodii."

"Let me try his room." This time the phone rang seven or eight times before it was picked up.

"Hello, Jade."

"Is this Jodii?"

"Yes."

"How did you know it was me?" I asked.

"Caller ID," Jodi responded.

"May I call you Jodii?"

"Yes, of course. How is the baby?"

"She's not a baby anymore. Ruby is six years old. Do you have time to talk?"

"Yes, of course." Jodii's voice was very soft and I could feel an immediate calmness come over me.

"Jodii, I have read Michael's journal."

"Where did you get it from?"

"Paul Curry sent me a copy."

"Oh, I see. What did you think of it?"

"Well, I was somewhat surprised and somewhat frightened."

"Yes, of course. I can see how the journal may concern you. So you have questions for me?"

"Yes. I think Michael is haunting Ruby."

"Haunting? No, Michael would not do that."

"Then what is going on with his connection to Ruby?"

"Jade, during my daily meditation I hear Michael's voice and I think I know what is happening. He died disaffected."

"What do you mean?"

"I believe he died with regrets."

"Regrets about what?"

"About the path taken."

"What path are you referring to?"

"If you read the journal you know about his obsession with the past and the future and his disconnection with the present. So he discovers Jost and Angel, his known pre-incarnates. Then he discovers Ruby, his reincarnated soul. But you recall how his life ended. He finds his true love Audrey, only to die shortly thereafter. I feel there is unfinished business that still needs to be resolved."

"Help me understand."

"I think he's searching for a vehicle to allow him to finish things up."

"Finish up what?"

"Finish up the present."

"I don't understand."

"Michael and Audrey were reunited. That happened after the journal was completed but just months before Michael's death. I believe Michael is disaffected over his child."

"Over Ruby?"

"No, over Su. Audrey has read the journal. She knows about you and she knows about Ruby. She and I have had many conversations about the seven of us meeting."

"Seven, what's seven?"

"You, James, Ruby, Paul, Audrey, Su, and me."

"Why have you not pursued this?"

"Audrey wants to be respectful of your privacy. She sees you as a person who has already been burdened by what Michael has done to you."

"First, I haven't been burdened by the marina he bequested me, and as for Ruby, I don't think it was Michael who selected Ruby to be his reincarnate."

"Well, that's a very open-minded and healthy perspective. But if you want this so called haunting to stop, I suggest that you at least have Ruby and Su meet."

"When?"

"Only you, James and Dr. Blink will know."

"Dr. Blink. Did he talk to you?"

"No."

"Then why did you bring him into the discussion?"

"I feel many things when I meditate and I hear his name when I meditate on Michael. Dr. Blink can be helpful. He may help you better understand Michael, Jost, and Angel. Keep Dr. Blink close."

"Jodii, what else could I be doing to move this

along?"

"I could have a friend of mine contact you."

"Who is your friend?"

"He is a retired monk. He lives in Cape Town. You may benefit from some meditation. He could help you find a quicker path to peace and relaxation."

"Let me think about it."

"Yes, of course."

"Jodii, thanks again for talking to me. I will be in contact."

"Have faith Jade, this will resolve itself." Then the call ended.

Chapter 13

Who is Calling Whom?

The next morning I updated James on my conversation with Jodii. James expressed caution about running off to America to meet with any of the seven. I, on the other hand, felt less cautious and more excited about the possibility of meeting Audrey, Jodii, and Su.

"James, what about meeting halfway?"

"What do you have in mind?"

"Well, we haven't been to the UK in quite a while. We could see your parents and my brothers, and then invite Audrey and Su to come over. We could meet out in the country at Little Wyndham. It would be perfect."

"Jade, I don't like the sound of it. It sounds kind of risky. What if things don't go well? If you want this meeting to happen, then maybe we should just go to the States. We could wrap it into a longer trip. First we could go home, then make a short trip to Iceland, then go to Virginia. On the return trip, we can stop in the Caribbean before starting the journey south."

"Sounds very complicated. I'll think on it."

Soon after, we sat down for breakfast. Ruby initiated the discussion. "Daddy, take me sailing today."

"Honey, I'm really busy today."

"Just a short sail in the harbor."

"James, that sounds like fun."

"No Mommy, I just want to go with Daddy."

"Why can't I go, Ruby?"

"I want to play a game."

"What kind of game?"

"I want Daddy to blindfold me. Then I want to see if I can steer the boat without seeing."

"Ruby, where did you get that idea from?"

"I'm not sure. I think I dreamt it."

"Did DataTwo tell you to do this?"

"No."

"Did Sunset tell you to do this?"

"Yes."

"Well, you tell Sunset, no thanks. Besides, the winds are up today and it is not safe to be out sailing in the harbor." Nothing else was said until Ruby left the room.

"Okay, James. How strange was that?"

"It was very strange. Do you suppose she read the journal?"

"No. She has no access to it. And besides, she's only six years old."

"I know, I know, but how else would she be able to know about Sonnet, Jost's sister?"

"I don't know unless she's been talking to her imaginary friends."

"James, has it occurred to you that maybe there are no imaginary friends at all? What if Michael Kenney is reading his journal to Ruby? Ruby's discovery of all these friends is following the chronology of the journal."

"Okay, that's an interesting theory. Should we test it?"

"No. Let's sit tight and see if something happens to any of her friends that would further support that theory."

Ruby had gone quiet again and I wondered if she did it to accommodate James and me or whether things had really calmed down. We were approaching another session with Dr. Blink and I was thinking that maybe it was time to share the journal with him, but James insisted that we sit tight on the issue, so I acquiesced.

Once again when we arrived at Dr. Blink's, the office was empty. I began to realize that this was intentional. He didn't want to be inconvenienced by other patients. The session started as it did before. Ruby took off her shoes and started her mental escape to the tree swing. Within a minute, Ruby was under the control of Dr. Blink.

"Ruby, how do you feel?"

"Fine."

"Is Michael there?"

"Yes. I am here, Dr. Blinkenstein." Blink looked over at his father's picture that hung on the wall beside his desk.

"Why did you call me Blinkenstein?"

"We all change our names, don't we?" Blink didn't reply.

"Michael, tell me what's bothering you."

"There are so many things."

"Tell me more," Blink suggested.

"I don't want to talk to you, Dr. Blink." Ruby's eyes remained shut.

"Who would you like to talk to?"

"Jade."

"Michael, you know I can't let you do that." There was no response. Blink said nothing. We sat for three minutes of silence as if Dr. Blink and Michael Kenney were playing a game of chicken. The only question was who would blink first. Then Ruby opened her eyes and stared at me. I squirmed in my chair and put my hand on James's arm.

"Talk to Michael," James whispered.

"Michael, how are you?" I felt like an idiot saying that to my child.

"I'm lost." A lump grew in my throat.

"Why are you lost?" I asked.

"You know why."

"Is it Audrey and Su?"

"Yes."

"What about them?"

"You know what has to be done."

"Tell me."

"I need to repair the damage."

"Michael, what damage?"

"Jade, you know."

"How do I know?"

"You talked to Jodii. You know what has to be done."

"Michael, I need some answers from you before I can help you." Ruby's eyes closed.

James leaned over to me. "What are you doing?" I ignored him.

"Michael, what about Ruby? Is she going to die like you and Jost?" Ruby opened her eyes.

"Don't know. Her soul is stronger than mine was. She will most likely be fine."

"You didn't answer my question, Michael Kenney. I have to know the answer to the question."

"Ruby will be fine, but …"

"But, what?"

"But, nothing."

"If I do what must be done, will you leave Ruby alone?"

"I didn't call her out."

"What are you talking about?" The tone of my voice was now showing signs of impatience.

"She called me."

"What are you saying?"

"It is Ruby that will not leave us alone. She wants me to resolve her issue. She calls out to me, and now she calls out to Jost, Angel and Sonnet. Our shared soul has been awakened. Why is she doing this? You know what has to be done. You know what has to be done. You know what has to be done. You know what has to be done."

"Michael, stop it!" Ruby went silent.

"Dr. Blink, end it now." Blink looked up as if he was just waking up from a deep sleep.

"Ruby, how is your swing?"

"Good."

"Okay, when I snap my fingers you will wake up." Blink leaned over to Ruby, placed his hand next to her ear and snapped his fingers. Ruby's eyes opened wide.

"Mommy, did I take a nap?"

"Yes, Ruby. Did you dream?"

"Yes."

"What did you dream about?"

"I had a dream that I had a sister."

"A sister?"

"Yes, she was an older sister. Mommy, she looked so pretty. She was tall and had yellow hair."

"Does she have a name?"

"No."

"If I say the name would you recognize it?"

"Mommy, she has no name."

I decided not to push the issue. As we walked toward the exit door of Blink's office, I felt a tap on my shoulder.

"Jade, call me in the morning and let's debrief."

I said nothing. I was too exhausted to reply.

Chapter 14

Lawyers, Locks and Keys

James and I pulled out a copy of Michael's journal and started to thumb through it. I felt as if there was a missing piece to the puzzle and the missing piece was Mickey Dermott. Mickey was Michael Kenney's attorney. He was the person I dealt with over Michael's bequest of Mac Delivery Service. Throughout the journal Mickey's name kept coming up. He was an important character in Michael Kenney's life; his adviser, his confidant, and close friend. Maybe a link could be made through Mickey Dermott? Maybe he would provide some insight into the Ruby/Michael connection?

Everything went quiet in the Morison household. There was no discussion about Dr. Blink, Michael Kenney, or any of Ruby's imaginary friends. Ruby had, in fact, slipped into a mode of normalcy. She was acting like every other kid in the neighborhood. She had made several new friends at school and appeared to have developed more interest in them than in DataTwo, Angel, Jost, or the sister she had dreamt about. In the meantime, I had contacted Mickey Dermott's law office and found out that Mickey had retired and was living in France. I was able to convince the administrative staff to surrender his email address and phone number. Later on in the day I decided to call his flat in Nice.

"Bon jour." The voice on the phone was male, so I dove right in.

"Mr. Dermott?" There was a long pause.

"Jade?"

"Yes, how did you know it was me?"

"I got an alert from my office in the States."

"I thought you retired from practice."

"Retired is a relative word. I've moved to Nice to deal with a very complicated legal issue. My client is over here so I decided to move here temporarily. So how have you been? How is the marina doing and how is that little girl of yours?"

"Well Mickey, some of these questions are easily answered. However, the question about Ruby is actually the reason for my call." Static began to appear on the line.

"Jade, please repeat your last sentence."

"I need to talk to you about Ruby."

"Oh, I see. Is she ill?"

"Good question; I honestly don't think so but I'm not sure." Then I launched into a fifteen-minute diatribe about the whole mess. Mickey never interrupted me. Finally when I was all done, Mickey re-engaged.

"As strange as it may seem, none of what you said

really surprises me."

"Why?"

"I don't know. I knew about Ruby's eyes; I saw the picture that you sent to Paul Curry. I had often wondered and sort of assumed that in some way Michael Kenney would creep back into your life, but I never actually pondered how that might happen."

"Let me ask you—do you still see or hear from Michael's wife, Audrey?"

"Sure, we are close friends."

"Has she ever said anything to you about her daughter having any strange experiences that would place a connection between her daughter and Ruby?"

"Let me tell you everything I know. Su was born six months after Michael's death. She is ten or eleven now and very pretty, sort of takes after her mother. She is tall for her age."

I interrupted him, "What about her hair?"

"Her hair is long, blonde, and straight. Su has always been smarter than the average kid. She started reading when she was three years old. She has excelled in school but in math and science, she's a total whiz. She's also a good athlete."

"What sport?"

"She plays tennis mostly but also ballet and gymnastics."

"What else? Anything about her health?"

"Define health."

"You know, is she sick a lot? Does she have any allergies or asthma or anything like that?"

"No." I could tell Mickey was holding back.

"Mickey, what is it? You know something. Come

on, give it up." There was a long pause.

"Okay; Su has a sleeping problem."

"Mickey, please stop the cat and mouse game."

"Okay; she has adolescent insomnia."

"When did it start?"

"I don't know, but it seems as if she has always had it."

"Do they know what causes it?"

"I think so."

"Tell me."

"Maybe you need to take this up with Audrey."

"Mickey, you've gone this far. Don't hold back on me now." There was another long pause.

"Su has a syndrome called night terrors."

"What is it?"

"Simply put, Su lives with terrible nightmares."

"What kind of nightmares?"

"I don't know."

"Is there anything that can be done for her?"

"I know Audrey keeps her room very cold. That seems to help. The doctor told Audrey that she probably will grow out of it."

"When?"

"The doctor said that sometime in her thirties, perhaps."

"Do you know if Audrey has ever thought about calling me or thought about getting our daughters together?"

"The topic has come up a few times."

"Why hasn't she pursued it?"

"That, you will have to ask her."

"How do you think she would react to a phone call

from me?"

"I don't know, but I don't think she harbors any bad feeling toward you. You should call her. Maybe you and Ruby are the key to resolving Su's night terrors."

"I was thinking the same thing."

"Look Jade, I have to run off to an appointment but would love to continue this conversation."

"Me too, but before you go, do you have Audrey's email address and phone number?"

"Yes. I'll have my office staff email it to you."

"Great. Thanks."

I gave him my email address, said goodbye and terminated the call. Later that day his email arrived. I sent the message to the printer and left the printed message on James's desk.

Chapter 15

Phone Bills

As I pulled another page from the calendar that hung on the wall of the marine office, I realized another month had drifted by. Somehow I just couldn't get myself to call Audrey. I thought about it so many times but the courage to do it never appeared. Then events began to change. By day's end, I talked myself into making the call. I took a deep breath, picked up the phone, placed it by my ear but heard no dial tone. There was silence on the other end. I could hear a crackling noise in the earpiece and decided to say something, but before I could, a voice appeared.

"Hello, hello."

The caller had a typical American accent. "Mac Delivery Service," I replied.

"Hello, I wonder if you could help me."

"Sure, go ahead."

"I'm trying to locate Jade Morison."

"This is she. Who am I speaking to?"

The crackling grew louder. "Jade, this is Audrey Kenney." The phone tumbled from my hand but I managed to grab it before it hit the floor.

"Audrey, I've been thinking about calling you."

"Yes, me too. This call is probably long overdue."

"How are you and Su?" I asked, as if we were best friends.

"We are fine. What about you?"

"Generally good but we've been having a few challenges with Ruby."

"Yes, I know."

"How do you know?"

"I keep close contact with Jodii."

I scrambled for something to say. "I had a long conversation with Mickey Dermott recently."

"I know. He told me all about Ruby."

"He did?"

"Yes, and he told me he had spoken to you and that he had filled you in on all of the issues regarding Su's night terrors."

There was an uncomfortable lull in the conversation. Then Audrey spoke up.

"Jade, have you looked at your phone bills recently?"

"No, why?"

"Do you have access to them online?"

"Yes."

"Can you pull them up?"

"Sure, give me a minute. Audrey, what's going on?"

"You'll see."

A minute later the phone bill appeared on the laptop. "My god!"

"That's what I said when I saw my bill. I think our girls have connected."

I scanned the dates and times. Each call was placed on the weekend at a time when Ruby would have had access to the landline. It seemed that both Audrey and I were so used to using our cell phones that we had basically ignored the landline bill. There were ten calls, all placed over a four-week period. The calls were long and the charge approximated 350 rands or $50 U.S. "Audrey, what do you know about this?"

"Nothing really. I wanted to talk to you first. There is one thing, however, that has occurred since the phone calls started."

"What's that?"

"Su has started to sleep through the night."

"You mean no more nightmares?"

"Exactly."

"That's strange because James and I have noticed that Ruby had settled down as well. She has not brought up anything about her imaginary friends and there has been no talk about Michael."

"Jade, do you suppose that they are the answers to each other's problems?"

"Maybe. So what's next, Audrey?"

"I don't know. I don't want to stop them, but at the same time, I don't like them doing this behind my back and certainly I don't like the phone bills. I wonder why they haven't used free video-conferencing."

"I don't know. We use Skype all the time."

"So do we. Maybe they want to keep their discussions private. I don't know. Let me think about it and I'll shoot you an email."

"Audrey, is it time for us to get together?"

"I think so, especially since the girls have found each other."

"By the way, do you have any idea who made the first call?"

"I don't know. Let's compare the phone call history."

I scanned the bills, giving Audrey dates and times. We determined it was Ruby who initiated the first call. We continued to talk for fifteen minutes. I told her all about the brief moments that I had experienced with Michael and she, in exchange, told me everything about her and Michael and their on-again off-again romance. The more we talked, the more I felt at ease with yet another person who had been woven into the life of Michael Kenney.

"Jade, we can all suffer from too much focus on the past and the future and in the final analysis, we may find that the present is just slipping through our fingers. The present is calling out to us and to our children. We need to answer its request and make a commitment to get together in the next few months."

"Okay. I'll think about the logistics and I'll email you next week." Then there was another lull in the conversation and I could sense that both of us were in tears. Seconds later, I heard a click sound, signaling that Audrey had terminated the call. I took a deep breath, wiped the tears from my eyes, and thought back to the day I printed the email from Mickey Dermott. I wondered if I subconsciously left it on James's desk so Ruby would discover it.

Chapter 16

Back to Blink

That night I updated James on the phone call from Audrey and the problem with the phone bills. He seemed neither excited nor upset about the issues. Then I ventured into dangerous territory. "James, I think we need one more session with Dr. Blink."

"Why? Things seem very much under control."

"I want to talk to Michael again."

"Jade, he wants to be left alone."

"How do you know?"

"He said so, remember?"

"What if he really didn't mean it?"

"Jade, why don't you ask Ruby? She seems to have all the answers."

"Hey, no need for sarcasm."

"Sorry, Jade. Look, why don't we just sit down with Ruby, confront her with the phone bill and find out what is happening between her and Su."

"No, I don't want to interfere with something that seems to be working for both of our girls."

"Jade, you said our girls like Su is yours and not Audrey's."

"I know how it sounds but I think there is something special going on here and I need to know what it is."

"Look, let's sleep on it and we'll talk about it in the morning. Okay?"

"Fine."

The notion of sleep was a myth. All night long I lay wide awake feeling the need to get one more chance to dialogue with Michael. I wanted to ask him or even interrogate him about who had awakened whom. I hadn't forgotten Jodii's comments, when he told me it was Michael who had unfinished issues to resolve with his wife and daughter. Then there was Michael's insistence that the unfinished business was between Ruby and Su. It all seemed so complicated and strange. After a while I started to doze, but was awakened by a piercing scream that originated from Ruby's room. I flew out of my bedroom and ran down the hall. Ruby was standing on her bed. Her eyes were closed but tears were pouring down her cheeks.

"Ruby, what's wrong?" She screamed again. Her eyes remained closed. I grabbed her and hugged her but it didn't seem to calm her down. "Ruby, wake up!" Then she opened her eyes.

"My name is Su!" Then she closed her eyes and collapsed in my arms.

I felt James's presence behind me. "Did you hear

that?"

"Oh yeah, I caught the whole thing. Maybe a trip to Dr. Blink is in order."

I put Ruby back to bed and returned to the bedroom. The next morning when Ruby woke up, I asked her about the nightmare and she said she had no recollection of it. "That was a good thing." I thought to myself.

That afternoon while I was at the marina, I called Dr. Blink and updated him on all of the events of the past weeks. He was very quiet and appeared disinterested. "Dr. Blink, I sense you are no longer interested in Ruby's health. What's up?"

"Jade, to be honest, I was a little uncomfortable after the last session."

"Did it freak you out, Dr. Blink?"

"Sort of."

"Well, it freaked me out too, but you can't abandon Ruby just because things got a little intense."

"Okay, what do you want," Blink replied in a voice of defeat.

"Put Ruby under one more time."

"What specifically are you searching for, Jade?"

"I want to know whether Ruby can reach into Su's consciousness and I want to resolve one of the contradictions that exist."

"And what is that?"

"Is this all about Michael and Su or about Ruby and Su?"

"Jade, have you ever thought that maybe it's everything, that there is no one dynamic at play? Personally, I think there is something going on with everyone Michael has touched. But if you want one more session, I'll do it under one condition."

"What's that?"

"You keep your cool, keep a level head and don't get angry with Michael Kenney or anyone else, living or dead. Can you agree to this?"

"Yes, Dr. Blink, I'll play by your rules."

"I'm free anytime next week. Just call the office and my assistant will get you an appointment."

"Thanks, Dr. Blink."

Then I hung up the phone and called home but the phone was busy. I thought for a second and called Audrey's number. Her line was also busy and I wondered if the girls were talking again.

Chapter 17

Too Many Questions

Problems at the marina began to show up when the diesel fuel tank at the fuel depot started to leak. Repairing the problem was paramount which meant that James was unable to accompany Ruby and me to Ruby's next session with Dr. Blink. When we arrived at Dr. Blink's office, there was a strange sense of confusion among the office staff. There were many patients sitting in the waiting room, most of them looking quite annoyed. As I was waiting to speak to the receptionist, the side door opened and Sara Bellim appeared.

"Jade, Dr. Blink will see you now."

I took Ruby by the hand and walked down the very familiar hallway. We entered Dr. Blink's office and sat there alone. Ten minutes later Dr. Blink walked in, accompanied by another man. The man was younger than Blink by at least twenty years, putting him somewhere between thirty-eight and forty-two years old.

"Jade, I want you to meet Dr. Benjamin Smoke."

I extended my hand. "Pleased to meet you." We shook hands but he said nothing.

"Dr. Smoke is a specialist in child psychology and hypnosis and has a keen interest in the paranormal."

"Ms. Morison, I hope you don't mind me observing during today's session?"

"Dr. Smoke, will you simply be observing or will you be involved in the session?"

"I would like to be involved but it's up to you. I have read Dr. Blink's medical file on Ruby. I have also reviewed his comments from the past two sessions, so I am very familiar with the case. I've also had several discussions with Jodii."

I rocked back in my chair trying to disguise my anxiety. "How do you know Jodii?"

"I have a connection to the monastery."

"Small world," I said.

"Yes, very small and very complicated."

By now I was beginning to feel uncomfortable with the dialogue that was occurring in front of Ruby. But as I glanced over at her I noticed she was reading a book that she had carried into Dr. Blink's office.

"Are you ready to start?" Dr. Blink asked.

"Almost," I replied. "Dr. Smoke, tell me about your conversations with Jodii."

"Do you want the short version or the long version?"

"Short will do."

"Jodii believes that we are very close to a breakthrough."

"Define breakthrough."

"He told me we are coming to a point where all things will be known."

"Did he say what kind of things?"

"Yes, he said we are very close to understanding the answers to our questions. This discovery will put into motion the actions that will resolve all the issues. He said you will be tempted to act emotionally and told me that much thought and contemplation must go into any decision involving Ruby."

I looked over at Ruby. She was still reading.

I called her name to get her attention but she was so involved with her book that she didn't hear me. I called her name again and once again, she did not respond. Finally I tapped her on the shoulder and she jumped as if she was being startled by a loud noise. Then the session began. Ruby quickly fell into a hypnotic state just as she had done before.

"Ruby, can you hear me?" Dr. Blink asked.

"Yes."

"Your mother is going to ask you a few questions. Is that okay?"

"Yes, Dr. Blinkenstein."

Then I started in. "Can I speak to DataTwo?"

"Why?"

"I have a few questions for DataTwo."

"What kind of questions?"

"Can you get DataTwo?"

"He doesn't want to be disturbed. He is tired. His work is done. My work is done."

I paused, not knowing where to take the conversation. Dr. Smoke moved his hand signaling me to continue.

"Michael, please talk to me."

"That's better. I don't like to be called DataTwo."

"Sorry, Michael. I spoke to Audrey. Are you happy that I did?"

"Jade, are you happy that you did?"

"Yes," I replied, realizing he was now on the offensive and that I was playing defense.

"The circle must be completed."

"What circle?"

"It is the circle of five."

"I don't understand."

"Jade, read the letter I left for you."

"I have read the letter."

"Then you know."

"Michael, just tell me."

"There are five people. Remember I told you about our destiny. I never defined 'our' in the letter. You have assumed 'our' meant you and me. Maybe it did, but it doesn't anymore."

I looked closely at Ruby. Her eyes were still closed and I was momentarily very uncomfortable listening to these words coming from Ruby's mouth in a little girl's voice. Dr. Smoke was taking notes while a tape recorder recorded the discussion.

"Michael, are you aware that Ruby and Su have talked?"

"Yes, they also dream about each other."

"No, I mean they have had actual discussions with each other."

"Don't leave phone numbers around."

"How did you know that?"

"I don't know why I know that, but no more questions. We must be five."

"Michael, is this really you?"

"Jade, is this really you?"

"Yes," I said, but received no reply from Michael. "Michael, I think the children will know what to do."

Then Ruby's mouth lipped the words "They will."

Dr. Smoke took a deep breath and signaled Dr. Blink to waken Ruby from her hypnotic state. Seconds later, Ruby was back and once again asked if we could get ice cream on the way home. I agreed.

Chapter 18

An Unfortunate Prediction

When the next morning arrived, Ruby was slow to get up. It was one hour passed her usual waking time. When she arrived in the kitchen, Ruby looked exhausted and disturbed.

"Good morning, honey," I said, placing my hand on her head.

"Mommy, I didn't like my visit to Dr. Blink's office yesterday."

"Why?" I said, with a hint of concern.

"Well, the visit was okay but the smell was back."

Now I stopped what I was doing and listened closely. "Ruby, tell me more. What did you smell?"

"Death."

"Where did you smell it?"

"What do you mean?"

"Well, did you smell it in the waiting room or in

the office?"

"I smelled it in the office near Dr. Blink. I think Dr. Blink is dead."

"Ruby, are you sure?"

"Yes, I had a dream about it. I saw him die in the hospital. The nurse said the word stoke."

"Do you mean stroke?"

"Yes, she said stroke, that was the word."

"Are you absolutely sure?"

"Yes. I was there with my sister."

"Your what?"

"I mean, by myself."

I didn't press the issue. Ruby walked to the table where she began eating her cold cereal and then lapsed into silence. I left the room and went to the phone with the intent to call the hospital. My call to the hospital was interrupted by the numbers that were showing on the auto-dial window of the phone. There was a display of a very long series of digits. The first digit was the long-distance code and the second, third, and fourth were the country code for the United States. I looked closely at the remaining numbers and quickly realized it was Audrey's number. The girls were at it again.

The hospital operator spoke in a very low voice. She sounded like a funeral director and for a brief moment I felt a chill come over me. "Excuse me, could you tell me if you have a patient named Blink in the hospital?"

"One moment. Let me check. Yes, we have a Dr. Blink."

"Can you transfer me to his room?"

"No, I'm sorry, he is in the ICU."

"Okay, can you transfer me to the ICU's nursing unit?"

"Sure, hold on."

The phone rang and was answered by a woman with a very harsh voice. "Hello, I was wondering about the condition of Dr. Blink."

"Dr. Blink passed away early this morning, shortly after midnight."

I could feel my heart accelerating. "Okay, thanks." I put the receiver down and fell back in the leather chair that was situated near the phone. I felt like crying, but for some reason I could not produce a tear. Then Ruby walked in the room.

"Mommy, was I right about Dr. Blink?"

"Yes, unfortunately you were correct."

"He didn't suffer. He just fell asleep."

"How did you know that?"

"It was all in my dream."

Ruby climbed into my lap, placing a head on my shoulder. I closed my eyes and wished she was two again, a time before she started speaking to shadows and before she found Michael Kenney. Later that day, I got a call from Dr. Smoke who informed me of Dr. Blink's demise. I told him that I knew, and how I knew and that Ruby predicted his death. Then he asked me if I was comfortable turning Ruby's care over to him. I thought about it for a split second and agreed. "By the way, Dr. Smoke, I would like to get a look at Ruby's medical records."

"Why?" he asked.

"I don't have to answer that. Let's just say I need to fully understand what Dr. Blink was really thinking about. I want to better understand why Dr. Blink wanted to abandon Ruby. I have to believe that there are some facts about these hypnotic sessions that will explain his actions."

"Fine, I will have my assistant prepare a copy for you. You should be able to pick them up next week."

"Thanks, I appreciate it."

"No problem. Let's talk next week after the funeral."

"Okay. I'll call you in your office." Then the call ended.

I decided not to go work, but rather to spend the day with Ruby. We drove down to the marina, walked by the office and went down to the slip where my father's boat was moored. We climbed aboard *Gem* and motored out of the marina. Within minutes we were under sail. I really loved sailing the old wooden Timberpoint in the inner harbor. It was a perfect boat for two people. I wondered about how it might feel if Michael was here on board with Ruby and me. I thought about questioning Ruby about Michael, but I didn't have to.

"Mommy, can I talk to you about Michael?"

"Sure."

"Michael feels bad about your discussion."

"What discussion?"

"Michael told me he talked to you."

"Really, when did he tell you that?"

"I don't know. He said he was sorry for being so mean to you. He said that he really likes us and he is grateful that you talk to him. He wants to do it one more time. He wants to tell you everything."

"How do I contact him?"

"I don't know, but do it like you did before."

"Ruby, are you sure you don't know how I talked to Michael?"

"No."

"Ruby, one last question? Why do you call Michael DataTwo? Is that his name?"

"Yes. DataTwo's real name is Michael."

"Ruby, what does DataTwo mean?"

"I don't know."

"Does it mean daddy number two?"

"Yes."

"Do you think he is your daddy?"

"No, he is Su's daddy."

"And how do you know that?"

"Su told me."

"When did she tell you that?"

"During our phone calls. Su told me that her mommy and you know about the phone calls."

"Yes, I know and why didn't you tell me about the phone calls?"

"I don't know. I just know I want to visit Su. Can we go visit her?"

"Yes, I think we should do that. I will talk to your father about it when we return to the marina."

Chapter 19

The Funeral

Dr. Blink's memorial service was the first Jewish service I had ever attended and by the sheer count of mourners, it was clear that Dr. Blink was a well-known and well-liked individual. James, Ruby, and I sat in the synagogue as a rabbi and other members of Temple Bethel recounted the glorious life of Dr. Blink. After the synagogue officials completed their memorial, others came to the podium to speak about the great Dr. Blink. The first person to step forward was a tall, lanky man who walked with a slight limp. He was fiftyish and introduced himself as Dr. Blink's private banker. He wore a hand-tied bow tie that sat slightly crooked around his neck. The dark gray suit he wore seemed appropriate for the weather and the occasion.

"Good afternoon, my name is Michael Maddocks. I am a longtime friend and adviser to Irving and will truly miss him. He loved his family, his profession, and his boat. When Irving died, he seemed to be in a bit of a transition. Yes, a transition, that's how he referred to it. He told me that over the last few months he had been working with a patient who gave him great insight into the value of his work and profession. This relationship provided hope for him and others and in some ways, Irving seemed both energized and yet a bit cautious about this transition. In the thirty years I knew Irving, I had never seen him so conflicted."

Then the banker paused and started looking for something as he checked the breast pocket of his suit. James leaned over to me and whispered, "Do you think Ruby is the patient that the banker is talking about?"

"I would bet on it," I replied. Then the banker pulled out several pieces of paper. I could see that the papers were handwritten. The banker cleared his throat.

"Irving gave this to me last week and asked me to read it aloud at his funeral. It is a bit long but that shouldn't be any surprise." Several members of the congregation chuckled, then the banker began.

> *"Good day to all. If all has gone as planned, I died two or so days ago. I wanted all of you to know that I died without fear or concern for myself, as I know what lies ahead of me. No doubt my death will be harder on my family and friends left behind than for me. So let me ramble on about what really matters. I've been very fortunate to have had a patient recently who provided me a glimpse of my future. Death is not the end, but rather a time to reconnect with those who have passed before. My wife who died several years ago*

has been waiting for me and as this letter is being read, we have already been reunited. Yes, life is so wonderful. My soul and all souls will be re-used—or perhaps 'given' is a better way to say it. I have kept a part of my soul or a copy of it to enjoy into eternity. And while much that I say is not consistent with my faith, I do believe it is reality as I now understand it. There are many jewels on Earth. They come in many colors. Most recently I have become very fond of red ones. Yes, life is full rubies."

I noticed the mourners looking puzzled. The banker then turned the page. James looked at me. "Hold on to your seat." He grabbed my hand. The banker continued.

"So let me be plain about it. Our souls are regenerated. The soul we possess while we live is a copy of a soul that had died before. I won't call it reincarnation but I guess in some respects it is. I have seen this firsthand and know beyond any doubt that it is true. So friends, rest easy about me and rest easy about yourselves. The future is planned and the future is bright, and I died a very happy man. There are a few people who I would like to recognize for their friendship and wisdom. First, let me thank someone not known to most of you, but who is known to just a few. This person—and I use this term very liberally—is a recent friend and confidant. His name is Michael Kenney."

The prayer book that was sitting on my lap fell to the floor. James squeezed my hand. "I knew it," I thought to myself.

> *"Over the past few months, I've been working with Dr. Smoke and through hypnosis I have had long discussions with this person who died several years ago. I have also hypnotized others who have connected with him."*

"That son of a bitch," I whispered to James.

The banker continued reading.

> *"I know what I have done may be looked at as being out of bounds but I tell you this in order to give all of you hope.*
>
> *Next, let me recognize the Morisons, who have looked after my boat, or the other woman, as my wife would call it. And then, of course, my family, friends and colleagues."*

Then the banker flipped to the last page.

> *"My family, my work, my friends, and my boat defined me. I've been blessed on Earth and now I am blessed in Heaven. Have a drink on me, have a sail on me, or whatever you do for pleasure, have it on me."*

The banker put the letter down and took a deep breath. "I'm really going to miss Irving. He was certainly an interesting and complex guy."

As Mr. Maddocks walked down from the podium, I leaned over to James. "Let's go."

"Jade, we can't just walk out.

"Do you want to bet!" And with that said, I stood up and walked out. James and Ruby followed. "James, I am so angry. Do you realize what he was doing?"

"Yes, I think so."

"Dr. Smoke hypnotized Blink and Blink called out

to Michael."

"Yes, and it also looks like Blink hypnotized Dr. Smoke for the same reason."

"No wonder Blink was feeling uncomfortable with me. He was afraid that Michael or Ruby would expose him."

Chapter 20

LaTeek

Several weeks later I got a call from Mike Maddocks instructing me to place a "for sale" sign on Dr. Blink's boat. He said he was appointed trustee for Dr. Blink's estate and that he would come by the marina to sign the listing agreement. We talked about the commission and settled on 10 percent. At noon, I walked to the slip where the late Dr. Blink's boat rested and placed the "for sale" sign on the bowsprit. As I walked down the dock, I took note of all the sailboats that we were collecting rent on and glanced up at the sky and once again thanked Michael for having provided this opportunity to James and me.

The rest of the day seemed to drift by as if I had napped through it. Then change came. I could hear a faint melody being hummed by a person who I thought was lurking just outside the marina office door entrance. The melody was familiar to me, as I had heard Ruby hum it many times before. I walked to the door, opened it and glanced down the pier. There was no one there. Then it started again. I walked outside and looked around the side of the building. The humming appeared to be getting louder so I walked to the rear of the building. There, sitting on a plastic storage box, was a middle-aged black woman. She was heavy, had dreads and wore a tattered flowered dress. She rocked back and forth as she hummed the familiar melody.

"Excuse me." The woman made no attempt to look my way. "Excuse me, what is that you are humming?"

"I don't know."

She still made no attempt to acknowledge my presence. "Where did you hear it?" I asked more forcefully.

"It came to me in a dream several months ago. It just came into my head."

"My daughter sings the same melody."

"Oh yes, I know."

"How do you know that?"

"I don't know."

There was a pause in the conversation as I searched for something to say. "My name is Jade."

"Oh yes, I know."

"How do you know that?"

"Your husband told me. My name is La Teek Akneequia, but feel free to call me La Teek."

"Nice to meet you, La Teek." I extended my hand but her hands remained on her lap. I looked at her closely, focusing in on her eyes. For a second I thought that maybe she had one blue eye and one brown eye, but that was not the case. I slowly squatted down and looked closely at her face, realizing that she was visually oblivious to me. Her eyes were amber and hazy and I realized that she was probably blind. "La Teek, are you blind?"

"Oh yes. They say I have cataracts."

"Why don't you get them fixed?"

"No need. I can see the world more clearly now."

"So is there anything I can do for you?"

"Oh yes. I have come here for a reason."

"What reason is that?"

"I'm not sure. I think I am looking for stones."

"What type of stones?"

"Red stones."

"La Teek, tell me more."

"Oh yes, there is much more to tell. You see, I am a wanderer. I have no home, no family, no friends, no money, no nothing. When I am cold, I find warmth. When I am hungry, I find food. When I am tired, I find rest and when I am sleepy, I find dreams. My dreams tell me where to wander and why. I dreamt of you in this place and I search for red stones."

"Tell me more about the red stones."

"There is nothing more to tell."

"La Teek, would you like to come inside the office where it is air-conditioned? I would be happy to get you a drink."

"Oh yes, water would quench my thirst."

I once again extended my hand but she ignored me. She simply stood up and walked ahead of me as if she could see perfectly. When she got to the entrance she reached out searching for the door handle but could not find it.

"Jade, my dear, would you help this old tired wanderer?"

I opened the door and guided her to a chair next to the water cooler.

"So Jade, tell me more about the red stones."

I hesitated to bring up the word Ruby so I played dumb and didn't respond to her request. Then the phone rang. It was Ruby.

"How was school today?"

"Good…" We talked about a minute. La Teek could sense that I was rushing to end the call as quickly as possible.

"Oh, so you have a child."

"Yes, a girl."

"What is her name?" I remained silent.

"She has no name?"

"Of course she has a name."

"What is it?"

"Ruby," I said reluctantly.

"Oh yes, my red stone."

Then La Teek reached into her pocket and pulled out a small leather pouch.

"This is for the little girl."

"What is it?"

"Inside the leather pouch are small square wooden tiles. Each tile has a letter on it. The tiles when put in a certain order will give you the answer to the question."

"To what question?"

"That, I don't know. Just give them to Ruby."

She tossed the pouch to me and I caught it with both hands as if I was catching a precious and breakable item.

"La Teek, please tell me more."

"There is nothing more to tell. I must go now. My work is done."

Then she started humming the melody again, stood up and walked out of the marina office. Seconds later she disappeared among the boats in the boatyard. I took the pouch, placed it in my pocket and walked down the dock looking for James. He was sitting on Blink's boat looking at a stack of papers that sat on his lap.

"Hey James, did you run into a black lady earlier today? She had dreads and looked like a homeless person."

"No, I didn't see anyone like that."

"That's weird."

"Come aboard and check this out."

"What are all those papers?"

"Well, I went down below to make sure that all was secure and these papers were sitting on the chart table."

"What do you think they are?"

"It appears to be Blink's journal. You were right about Blink. He and Dr. Smoke were routinely trying to talk to Michael through the power of hypnosis. Check this out." James handed me a page of the journal. There were several paragraphs talking about the replacement. There were also references made about Su, Ruby, Michael and me. I gave the papers back to James and then updated him on my visit with La Teek.

James wanted to see the pouch. He opened the pouch and poured the letters on the deck. He turned each one face up and tried to spell out the word replacement but the letters didn't match up.

"James, let's take the journal home and we will review it tonight."

"Better yet, take it to the office and make a copy and I'll put the original back where I found it. My guess is that Dr. Smoke will be looking for it."

"Good idea."

Chapter 21

Stories Not Told

Later that evening James and I sat together in the living room reviewing the document that he had found on Dr. Blink's boat. There were two separate documents that were somewhat unrelated. One was a sort of chronology about his life starting back when he was in elementary school and ending about a year ago. Most of the information was highly summarized and in only a few instances did Dr. Blink get into any detail. Of particular interest was an on-again off-again battle with insomnia and night terrors, very similar to what was plaguing Su.

It appeared that Dr. Blink took a medical approach by taking several drugs which he referred to as his sleep cocktail. But the combination of drugs had several side effects, one of which was night terrors. He mentioned that the drug combination was sometimes used to treat

Tourette's Syndrome. He also revealed in his writings a battle that he had with introversion. Dr. Blink preferred to be alone. He derived more pleasure from his own company than through the company of others. This led to many shallow relationships in his life. This may have explained why he always sailed alone. There were a few comments about experimentation which dated back some forty years, and James and I wondered if the experiment was a general reference to Blink having tried illegal drugs or maybe hallucinogens. There was very little said about his wife and son, nothing about his parents, and just one reference about his dog.

The other document, which covered the last year or so, was quite revealing and written in a fair amount of detail. Dr. Blink was aware of his pending death. He had been diagnosed with severe heart disease that was deemed to be untreatable unless a heart transplant could be performed. Donor hearts were hard to come by and artificial hearts were still considered experimental in South Africa. Prior to his sessions with Ruby, he was engaging in exhaustive hypnotic sessions. These sessions were orchestrated by Dr. Smoke. Blink believed that through hypnosis he could cure his insomnia, see his past more clearly and even see the edge of the future. These hypnotic sessions would generally last for several hours but occasionally he would stay under the hypnosis spell for days. What Dr. Blink didn't know was what form the future would take. It wasn't until Ruby and I came on the scene that he began to understand that beyond the immediate future was a distant future. He called the time and space of Michael Kenney the distant future. He never understood how souls were transferred and how souls were made. He first tried to reach Michael Kenney shortly after our first session with Ruby, but there was no response. Then there were second and third attempts but no response from Michael. The fourth time he tried, he did get a response from Michael, but it was only two words: Bala Nataraja. Dr. Blink believed that this name may have been a person whose soul was shared with him. He made Dr. Smoke put him under and tried to have Bala speak to him through Dr. Blink but the only words that were spoken were, "Yes I am." Dr. Blink wanted more so he put Dr. Smoke under and interrogated him. The only response from Bala was "Yes I am." Over time, Dr. Blink became jealous of Ruby and me as he wanted to have the kind of dialogue with Bala that we had with Michael. In the end, Dr. Blink found the answer to his questions not through hypnosis but through his dreams. He discovered that Bala was a doctor living in India who died two years to the day prior to Dr. Blink's birth. While it came to him in his dreams, the date of Bala's death was verified by the Department of Vital Statistics in New Delhi.

Then Dr. Blink's writings turned to discussions about the replacement and how it would impact Ruby and Su. He mentioned that he had dreamt about the replacement and that it was confirmed by discussions he had with Michael while dreaming. He said that the replacement was perfect in every way. He said it was a fulfillment of Michael, the essence of Michael, and his replacement. The replacement was the answer for Ruby and Su, for me and for all.

The whole concept bothered me but bothered

James much more. I could tell that James was starting to feel threatened by the concept of the replacement. He stopped reading and left the room. I continued on until I came to the last line of the journal, which simply said, "I need to tell Jade about La Teek."

Chapter 22

Re-grounded

It took two weeks for James to get re-grounded. He had grown very negative and resentful of Dr. Blink, Dr. Smoke, Michael, Su, Audrey, and me. He had put his foot down about traveling to the States to see Audrey and Su. As part of a compromise, I agreed to seek a new pediatrician not associated with Dr. Blink and to slow down the discussion about going to the U.S. The visit from La Teek was never discussed again and I didn't let James know that Blink had mentioned her on the last page of his journal.

Then there were the wooden tiles that sat inside the small leather pouch. I decided not to give them to Ruby as La Teek had suggested. Instead, I kept them out of sight. I did decide to keep a log of every new person I'd met and after I got a few names, I would take out the tiles and try to assemble names from the letters, but I had no luck.

After a few months had passed, James had forgotten about the replacement issue, so I approached him on the topic of the visit to see Su and Audrey. James thought that maybe it was time to go and encouraged me to contact Audrey to finalize the plans. However, it was his parting shot that left me cold.

"Jade, I won't be traveling with you and Ruby. I'm done with this Michael Kenney issue."

"James, come on, don't be that way."

"Look, Ruby has been fine for months. There have been no nightmares, no talking to shadows, no imaginary friends, her grades are good, and other than the long-distance phone bill, she is finally normal. So go to the States, have a great time with the girls but keep me out of it."

"James, please reconsider."

"Jade, I have a marina to run, bills to pay, and very little time. You and Ruby go and have fun."

"No James, I'm not going without you."

"Okay then, suit yourself."

"James, please."

"No Jade, I've supported you on this wild goose chase from the beginning, but it's over." And with that said, he turned his back and walked away. I was dumbfounded. In all the years James and I were together I had never seen him act so uncompromising and never heard him talk to me in such an apathetic tone. I was truly at a loss for what to do.

For the next three days James and I remained cool toward each other and I wondered if he was falling out of love with me. His relationship with Ruby and everyone else seemed normal, so I knew I was the source of his coolness. We started to drive in separate cars as we both headed off to the marina, and I felt like my marriage was crumbling. At noon the next day, James walked into the marina office and sat down at one of the desks. He cleared his throat as if he was going to deliver a speech and he began.

"Jade, we need to find a compromise, a win-win. I'm really okay with you going to the U.S. to see Audrey and Su. I just don't want to go."

"Is it the money, James?"

"No, I just think you'll have more fun with me out of the way. I'll be the fifth wheel, the odd person. I really think you would be better off alone. So here's the compromise. I'll fly with you and spend a day or two with you and Audrey, then I'm going off on my own to do some business."

"What kind of business?"

"Well, there is a convention of marina operators in Newport, Rhode Island. There's a boat show in Annapolis, Maryland, and I have an opportunity to crew on race boats both in Newport and in Annapolis. I'll swing back to Hampton, spend a day or so at the end, and then we can travel back to South Africa. On the way back maybe we could make a stopover in the UK and see my parents. We'll make it a three-week trip."

"What about Ruby and her school work?"

"We'll pull her out for the three weeks. She can catch up when we return; she's a smart kid. So what do you think?"

"It sounds doable. It's a reasonable compromise and if nothing else, it will get us back on speaking terms."

"I'm sorry that I've been so stubborn but it's time to

put the stubbornness aside and move on."

"It is great to have you back, James."

"Thanks. So how about we go down to Blink's boat and fool around?"

"Really, how can I pass that up?"

"You can't."

An hour later we emerged from Dr. Blink's boat, happy, satisfied, tired, and deeply in love.

"Hey, maybe we should fight more often, because the making up part is really great."

"James, don't press your luck."

We both laughed and went about our day.

Chapter 23

Tiles

Ruby came running into the kitchen holding the wireless phone.

"Mommy, Audrey wants to talk to you."

"Hi, Audrey, how are you?"

"Great, Jade, how's life treating you?"

"Very well, thanks."

"How are the trip plans?"

"We have our tickets booked, James has made all his plans and everything looks good."

"Have you thought any more about the meeting of the seven of us?"

"No, I don't think it will need to happen."

"Why, you told me Michael said it was essential."

"Well, there have been a few other things that have gone on recently regarding the death of Dr. Blink and this mysterious woman who showed up at the office."

"What about her?"

"She gave me a bag of small wooden tiles. Each tile has a letter on it. I think the letters, when properly arranged, will resolve all of the unknowns in our lives."

"Jade, how can that be?"

"I'm not sure but I have a hunch that we will be best served by living our lives as normally as possible."

"Interesting you say that. Su has gone three months without any sleeping problems."

"Same for Ruby. No imaginary friends and no odd behavior. Somehow the girls have found peace with their lives through each other. Audrey, let me ask you a very strange question."

"Sure, go ahead."

"Do you think that there is another Michael out there?"

"Do you mean another man for me to love?"

"I guess so. I mean, do you think there is another person out there whose soul is connected to Michael, as if Michael was not the only person who had the soul of Jost and Angel."

"I don't know. Maybe there are others."

"In Dr. Blink's journal he said something about a replacement. I wonder if he meant a replacement for Michael, someone who was a part of him, someone who you might think was Michael."

"You know, Jade, anything is possible."

"Have you met any new people lately?"

"No, not really."

"Well if you do, email their names to me. I want to see if the letters spell their name."

"What about women's names?"

"Sure, email those to me as well."

"Okay, it sounds weird, but what the heck."

"Look, Ruby wants the phone back."

"So does Su. I'll call you next week to firm up our plans."

"Great, talk to you later."

"Okay, bye."

Later that day while I was preparing dinner, Ruby started humming that melody again.

"Ruby, where did you learn that song?"

"I dreamt it."

"In your dream, who taught it to you?"

"I think she was a homeless person."

"Do you remember anything else about her?"

"I think she was blind."

"Really? Does she have a name?"

"Yes."

"Do you remember it?"

"No, but I think it's a boat name."

"What do you mean?"

"You know, like a part of the boat: like sail, rope, or tiller, something like that."

"What about wood?"

She thought for several seconds. "Her name was Teak!"

"Have you ever seen her outside your dreams?"

"No."

"Stay here for a moment." I went into the bedroom and returned with the tiles. "Ruby, do you know what this is?"

"No, tell me."

"Here, open the pouch."

"Letters?"

"Yes. You make words with them."

"What kind of words?"

"Any kind. Make words from the letters and write them down. Make as many words as you can."

"Okay."

"And Ruby, please take care of them. They are very special and very important."

Ruby took out a piece of paper and started. By the time I was ready to set the table for dinner, she'd made forty words, none of which was very illuminating. Later that night after Ruby had gone to bed, I decided to try my luck. I first took out the letters and arranged them in alphabetical order. AAABDKIMNOST. Then I started to stare at them. What was Michael trying to say with these tiles? What did Dr. Blink mean by replacement? For the next hour I tried to match the names of all the new people I had met over the last several months to the letters, but came up empty-handed.

Chapter 24

John

The traffic that piled up outside Johannesburg airport should have been an indication of what lay ahead but the excitement of the trip tended to overshadow any concerns. The trip required seventeen hours of flying time, plus a short stopover in Frankfurt, Germany, making the whole excursion twenty hours. We did pick up six hours in time zone changes and somehow I convinced myself that it was only an eleven-hour trip. After clearing the ticket area we proceeded to security, which given the state of world affairs, seemed very cursory. We reclaimed our carry-on baggage and walked to the gate awaiting the boarding process. I had noticed that Ruby was a little antsy, which I attributed to the general excitement and her anticipation of seeing Su the next day.

"Mommy, do you see that man over there?"

"Where?" Ruby pointed toward the security area.

"Honey, what are you pointing at?"

"See that man with a white shirt just walking out of security?"

"Yes, what about him?"

"He keeps looking at me."

"Ruby, I think it's your imagination."

"No, Mommy, he was standing in line next to me and he kept looking over at me. Then he looked at me again in the security area."

I looked over toward him, only to catch him looking away as if I had caught him in the act. "Ruby, just ignore him."

"Mommy, he's looking at us again." This time, I looked up and caught him. We made eye contact and he smiled as if he was saying hello. At that moment, James returned from the men's room and sat down beside me.

"Do you see that guy sitting at the end of the row?"

"You mean the guy in the white shirt?"

"Yes."

"Do you know him?"

"No. Ruby says he keeps staring at her."

"Ruby, don't worry about him. Think about the trip."

Then he stood up and walked toward the newsstand. He was tall, trim and quite good-looking. My guess was that he was in his early fifties. He carried a brown leather briefcase and had the look of a doctor or lawyer. He then disappeared into the crowd. Ten minutes later, the boarding process began. We were seated in a three-seat row. James took the window seat, Ruby took the middle, and I took the aisle. The opposite aisle seat remained empty. Then just as the flight attendant was ready to close the door, the man Ruby was complaining about walked onto the plane. He walked slowly toward us and nestled into the seat opposite me. I avoided eye contact, casting my eyes onto the in-flight magazine that I had picked up moments earlier. Then the plane started to roll back. The flight attendant began her rundown of all the typical safety protocols. The pilot informed us that we were number three for takeoff and ten minutes later we were airborne. It took less than five minutes before James fell asleep and less than six minutes before Ruby started elbowing me.

"Mommy, what is that man doing sitting by us?"

"I don't know."

"I want to move."

"That won't happen, so forget about it."

"Okay." Soon Ruby fell into a deep sleep as evidenced by her breathing. Then I felt a tap on my arm. I looked over. It was him.

"I'm sorry to bother you, but have we met before?"

"No, I don't think so."

"Your daughter looks very familiar to me."

"She said you kept staring at her."

"Staring may be a bit of an exaggeration, but she just looks very familiar. I noticed her eyes are quite unique."

"Yes, we hear that a lot."

"Do you live in Johannesburg?"

"No, we live in Cape Town. And you?"

"I live in the States but I come to South Africa frequently."

"What brings you here?"

"Wine. I am a co-investor in some vineyards in Franschhoek."

"That's a beautiful area."

"Yes, I really like it there. I am thinking of buying a house in the Valley but want to stay fairly close to Cape Town."

"Why is that?"

"I have a real passion for sailing and I would like to buy a small boat."

"Very interesting. So where are you heading?" I asked.

"New York, and you?"

"Virginia. I'm going to see a friend."

"That's a long trip for a friend; she must be very special."

"Yes, you could say that."

"Are you sure we haven't met before?"

"I'm very sure."

"By the way, my name is John."

"I'm Jade."

"And your daughter and husband?"

"Ruby and James."

"Nice family."

"Thanks, and what about you—any family?"

"No, just me; no siblings, no wife, no children."

He said it in a very sad way as if he had longed for more than what he had experienced in life. Then he got up from his seat and moved to the back of the plane.

Moments later, my eyes grew heavy and I, too, fell into a deep sleep. It was a sunny day and activity around the marina seemed very light. John appeared at the entrance to the marina office and walked in. He looked more handsome than he looked when we had met in the airport. He grabbed my hand and led me from behind the counter. I wanted to say something to him but I was unable to talk. We walked outside the marina office and started the long walk down the main pier. He grabbed my hand in a way that was slightly seductive, and I felt happy that he had. I could feel the sun warming my back and felt like I was walking on air. In the background I could hear birds sing the melody that was so familiar. John continued to guide me toward the end of the pier where Dr. Blink's boat lay.

"John, why are we here?"

"Isn't this what you want?"

"I don't know."

We went onboard and then went down below. La Teek was sitting in the salon. She was staring into space and humming the melody. I turned to John, but he was gone.

"La Teek, where did he go?"

"My child, do not fear him. Let him in, let him in."

Then I looked behind me and he was back. I reached out and took his hand and guided him to the forward bunk. I looked back toward the salon and gasped for air as La Teek was replaced by James.

Then I forced my eyes open and escaped from my dream. I thought for a moment about what had just happened and regretted James's appearance in the dream. I rearranged my pillow and fell back asleep.

We were sailing. John was at the helm. The winds were blowing just enough to move the boat through the still waters. I looked up at him and felt in love in the same way I had felt about James when we first met. I stood up and kissed John on the lips and we embraced. We stayed together for what seemed like hours, all while the strange melody played in the air. Then I looked up at John and he said, "We are one."

Chapter 25

Another Ghost

I was awakened by the voice of the pilot indicating that we would be experiencing some bumpy air and that all passengers should return to their seats. I looked over at James and Ruby, who remained fast asleep, and wondered where their dreams had taken them. I turned and looked toward the rear of the plane hoping to see John, but he was not in my line of sight. One half hour later, we had passed through the bad air and the restriction was lifted, so I got up, left my seat and walked to the rear of the aircraft hoping to spot John. I walked very slowly scanning each row looking for him but found no John. Then I spotted an empty seat just ahead and wondered if John had possibly walked to the restroom. I approached the empty seat and noticed John's briefcase tucked under the seat in front of the empty one. Lying on the seat was an immigration form. It was face up and I could easily read the information handwritten on the document: John Lyr, 301 South Main Avenue, Albany, New York. I took out my pen and wrote the information on my hand and then walked back to my seat. James and Ruby were still in a deep sleep.

I decided to take advantage of the in-flight WiFi and booted up my laptop. Then I went searching. First I did a search on Albany, New York. The search came back with lots of information but the only information I wanted was population. Then I went to people-search and searched for John Lyr, Albany, New York. No hits came back on that search. Then I went to ancestry.com and searched for Lyr. But no hits were found there either. I was dumbfounded. Maybe he wasn't an American, though I recalled seeing the U.S. citizen box checked on his immigration form. Next I searched on U.S. vital statistics and was taken to a government site listing all people in the U.S. retirement system, SSA (Social Security Administration.) Like the other sites, there was no Lyr to be found. I thought back to Michael Kenney and wondered whether I had encountered another ghost. How could there be no record of this person? Who was John Lyr and what was his fascination with Ruby? I kept searching.

For ninety minutes, I searched every keyword possible and still came up with nothing, so I logged off the Internet and put the computer away.

Soon after, James and Ruby awakened. "So how are my sleepyheads?"

"Good," Ruby replied in the middle of a yawn.

"And you, James?"

"Okay," signaling with a thumbs up.

"Mommy, I have to go to the bathroom."

"Okay, I'll take you." Ruby and I slipped out of our seats and started walking toward the front of the plane. As we approached the forward restrooms, we were stopped by the flight attendant.

"Excuse me, these toilets are for first-class passengers only. You will have to use the toilets in the rear of the aircraft." I said nothing, though I'm sure the flight attendant could tell by the expression on my face that I was not happy about her instructions.

"Come on, Ruby, let's go to the back of the plane." We walked carefully, making sure we didn't bump any passengers, the majority of which were sleeping. Then Ruby stopped dead in her tracks. She turned around.

"Mommy, there is that man."

"I know, and by the way, his name is John."

"Okay, but I don't want to walk passed him."

"Ruby, it looks like he is sleeping."

"I don't care."

"Ruby, okay, I'll go first." I led the way passed John until we got to the toilets. Then Ruby went into the first available toilet and I stayed outside the door, repositioning myself so I could keep one eye on John. He remained asleep in his seat. Once Ruby emerged from the toilet, we walked back toward our seats, once again making sure we didn't disturb any of the other passengers. When we returned to our seats, James appeared to be more awake and eager to engage in conversation.

"So what have you been doing while I've been sleeping?"

"Nothing, really."

"Jade, I saw you using the laptop."

I hesitated to tell him as I didn't want Ruby to hear the conversation. "I'll tell you later."

"I'm sure I can guess." And by the look on his face, I could tell he already knew what I was up to.

"Ruby, would you like to watch a movie? Let me put on your headphones and see what in-flight movies there are that you might like to watch." We scanned through the movie list and selected a movie. Moments later, Ruby was fully engaged in the movie so I turned to James, but before I could say anything, he spoke up.

"So let me guess. The guy that was bothering Ruby has a name which you have discovered. Did he tell you or did you steal his wallet? Well, somehow you found out his name, then you searched the Internet to find out something about him but found nothing."

"I didn't steal his wallet but I did see his immigration form, and, yes, I have been searching the Internet seeing what I could find out about him."

"So what did you find?"

"Nothing, like he doesn't exist."

"Why do you care?"

"I don't know, I guess…" James interrupted me before I could finish my sentence.

"Let me guess. Somehow you think he is related to Michael Kenney."

"No, I wasn't thinking that way but it appears that maybe I should."

"Hey, sorry for the sarcasm. Let me out. I need to go to the restroom."

I stood up and let James out. When he returned, I looked at my watch and realized he'd been gone for half an hour.

"Where have you been?"

"Well, I bumped into your mystery man. He is a very interesting guy. I'll fill you in on our conversation and my observations a little later."

Chapter 26

Pack of Lies

Ruby paused the movie as the flight attendant passed lunch boxes to each of us.

"So Jade, what did you learn about John?"

"Okay, he has no family, lives in the United States in a place called Albany in New York, he has invested in vineyards in the Valley, likes sailing, and is a U.S. citizen (according to his immigration papers.) However, I could not find anything about him on the Internet and there was no reference at all to his last name and that's after having checked out thirty sites. And what did you find out, James?"

"Much of the same, except there is one odd thing about the fact pattern."

"What's that?" I asked, feeling surprised that I missed something.

"You obviously didn't study his hands."

"What about them?"

"He is wearing a wedding ring."

"Really; I missed that."

"Apparently so."

"Anything else?"

"He is an artist."

"Professional artist?"

"No, amateur I think, though he did mention that he had sold some pieces."

"How did you discover that?"

"Well, he told me about his interest in sailing and I asked him if he had any other hobbies. That's when he told me about his artwork. Oh, and one other thing."

"What's that?"

"He drives a Saab."

"How do you know that?"

"He had his keys lying on the tray table. I saw this Saab key."

"Oh, that's weird."

"Well, what's even weirder is the key was old. I asked him what kind of Saab used that type of key and he said it was from a Sonett."

"Oh James, that is way too weird."

"I know."

"Would it be strange if it was Michael's car?"

"I wanted to ask him where he got it, but I didn't want to hear the answer."

"Well, I do want to know." And with that, I got up and walked back to talk to John.

When I arrived at his seat, I noticed that the seat across from him was temporarily vacant, so I sat down and moved right into the interrogation.

"John, got a minute?"

"Sure."

"James told me you have an old Saab Sonett. A friend of mine had a yellow Sonett and I know those cars are very rare. What color is yours?"

"Green."

"Was it ever yellow?"

"No."

"Where did you get it?"

"It's been in my family since it was new. My father bought it new and gave it to me in the 1980s."

"Did you ever know a Sonett owner named Michael Kenney?"

"No, the name is not familiar to me."

"Are you sure?"

"Very sure."

"One last question. You said you have no family?"

"That's what I said."

"Well, why are you wearing a wedding ring?"

"It belonged to my father."

"Really. It doesn't look that old."

"Believe what you want. Any more questions?" he said in an irritated voice.

"No, thanks for talking to me," and with that, I got up and walked back to my seat. When I arrived, Ruby was watching the movie and James was reading a sailing magazine.

"So Jade, what did you find out?"

"He got the Saab from his father, he never heard of Michael Kenney, and the wedding ring belonged to his father."

"That it, anything else?"

"Yes."

"What?"

"He is lying about the ring. That ring was not his father's."

"How do you know?"

"John is about fifty-five or so. That ring is a modern design. I bet it is only twenty to twenty-five years old. There's something about him that I don't trust. He's hiding something."

"Do you really think so?"

"Absolutely, and I'll figure it out before too long."

"I suggest you leave him alone."

"I will. I have enough information." I took out my laptop and went back to the Internet and started to search. Hour after hour, I searched but no leads were appearing. By now I was growing frustrated and decided to go in a different direction. I put my laptop away and turned to Ruby.

"Honey, how was your movie?"

"It was good. Can I watch another one?"

"Sure, but first I want to talk to you about that man we met in the airport."

"Why?"

"I'm just curious."

"I know a lot about him," Ruby said.

"You do?"

"Yes. I dreamt about him."

"What do you know?"

"He had a wife and two children."

"Ruby, tell me more."

"They are gone."

"What do you mean, gone?"

"I don't exactly know. In my dream I saw him wave goodbye to them."

"Where were they?"

"I don't know."

"Anything else you want to tell me?"

"He was very sad."

"And what about the others, how did they look?"

"I don't know, they had no faces. They were like puppets or something like that."

"Anything else?"

"No, can I watch the movie now?"

"Sure."

Minutes later, I was back on the Internet doing obituary searches but found no information that would support Ruby's dreams.

Chapter 27

The Great Divide

The descent and landing into Frankfurt airport was flawless. Like always, the deplaning seemed to take a long time as people gathered their luggage and personal items. Once out of the gate area, we moved over to the side and started to reorganize our carry-on bags as we needed to find our boarding passes for the next leg of our flight.

"So where are you going next?"

I looked up. It was John. "We are heading to Dulles in Washington, D.C., and you?"

"JFK in New York."

"Well, I guess this is the great divide."

"I guess so," he said, as if disappointed we were not sharing the next leg.

"Hey, if you get to Cape Town and are looking for a great used boat, look us up."

"Okay, I will."

"James, do you have a business card?" James reached into his pocket and gave the business card to John.

"Mac Delivery Service? Who is Mac?"

"He was the former owner."

"Thanks. I hope to see you in Cape Town sometime."

"Thanks; me too." We shook hands and walked away.

Our four-hour layover went by quickly and before we knew it, we were boarding the plane for our flight to the U.S. The plane was surprisingly empty for an international flight, so I took advantage of it and moved into a row by myself. Shortly after takeoff a flight attendant came by.

"Can I get you something?"

"Yes, I'll have a glass of red wine." She handed the small wine bottle to me and I noticed the vineyard was from Franschhoek. I thought how unusual it was to have local South African wine on the U.S.-bound flight and especially on a U.S. owned airline. I peeled off the label and studied it and then put it in my purse for future reference. Then I noticed the wine buzz approach and an involuntary grin came to my face. I started to think about John, almost fantasizing about him, and wondered if he was having the same thoughts of me. I closed my eyes and started to dream.

The sign in front of the building said M. S. Vineyards. I was in Franschhoek. Dr. Blink's boat was lying on its side in the middle of the road. Small monkeys were jumping from the roof of the building to the boat. The monkeys had no faces. Zebras were grazing on the land beside the building but instead of being black and white, they were yellow and green. The monkeys started to sing the familiar song that La Teek and Ruby hummed. Michael Kenney appeared and was carrying a ceiling fan and then disappeared. The monkeys started to ride the zebras and now the zebras were starting to sing the song as well. Then John appeared and started to sing the song. One of the monkeys walked up to me. He had a regular monkey face. He grabbed my hand and started walking with me.

"Come inside and meet the family."

"What family, Mr. Monkey?"

"The family of M. S.," the monkey replied.

I took the monkey's hand and started to walk toward the building. Now La Teek stood in the doorway. She had a monkey on her head and the monkey had a tiny zebra in his arms. I looked down to the monkey that was guiding me toward the house.

"What is your name, Mr. Monkey?"

"Michael Kenney, of course." I said nothing.

As we walked, the house got farther away. "Monkey, will we meet the family?"

"Oh yes," the monkey said, in the voice of La Teek.

"Come on, hurry," John screamed. We started to run until we got to the door.

The inside of the building looked like a typical vineyard tasting room. Everywhere I looked there were bottles of wine and every bottle was marked M.S. except one. Rather than an M.S., there were two words, one starting with an "M" and the other starting with an "S." I reached for the bottle to read the words but before I could, a monkey grabbed it and ran away with it. I tried to run but my feet were stuck to the floor. Then John appeared.

"Jade, would you like to meet my family?"

"Yes, of course."

He extended his hand and I grabbed it. My feet became unstuck. My heart was racing. We walked through another door and into a cold dark room. I could see people standing in the shadows but I couldn't see their faces.

"John, my love, I can't see them." John released my hand and walked over to the wall. Then he flipped on the light switch and the room became illuminated.

"Jade, meet my family."

There were three mannequins, each one standing against the wall. They were undressed and faceless.

"Jade, these are my wife and children."

I extended my hand, thinking it was the right thing to do. The woman mannequin's hand came to mine. I grabbed it and shook it, but all I could do was stare at her wedding ring.

"John, what is her name?"

"Audrey."

"And your children?"

"Su and Ruby."

"Why are they not real?"

"They are dead."

"How did they die?"

"That I can't tell you."

"Who is M.S.?"

"That I can't tell you."

"Why did you bring me here?"

"That I can't tell you." Then John screamed, "Wake up! Wake up!"

I forced my eyes open and out of my dream. "Jade, are you okay?"

"I was having a nightmare."

"No kidding," he said sarcastically. "You were talking in your sleep and really drawing a lot of attention to yourself, not to mention scaring Ruby."

"James, I think I was just in the Twilight Zone."

Chapter 28

Wheels Down

While the customs and immigration process at Dulles Airport seemed to take a long time, the flight from Dulles to Newport News was gone in the blink of an eye. I had told James about my nightmare and all he could do was remark about monkeys, zebras, and boats, a takeoff of lions, tigers, and bears, a quote from the "Wizard of Oz," and a phrase often used by James to describe a list of items. The walk from the gate and passed security went quickly and as we approached the terminal, I could see Audrey and Su standing there. While I had never met them in person before, I knew it was them.

Ruby started running toward Su and seconds later, they embraced. Their embrace was magical. Then they walked to the side and away from Audrey and began talking. I could see Audrey inch up to the security area and as I passed by the gate, we greeted each other with a long embrace.

"Audrey, I am so happy to finally see you in person."

"Me too. You're just how I pictured you."

"Audrey, this is James." James and Audrey hugged and in an uncustomary way, James's shyness toward other women did not show through.

"Ruby, come meet Audrey." But she didn't reply.

"Let the girls get acquainted. We'll have plenty of time for introductions."

It was a short walk to the baggage area and I noticed that James couldn't take his eyes off of Audrey.

"James, she's so pretty."

"Absolutely. Pretty is an understatement."

"So how was your trip? You must be exhausted," Audrey said.

"It was fine, a bit long, but we all slept a lot. I have to tell you about the crazy dream I had."

"I can't wait to hear about it."

Soon the bags arrived so we loaded them into Audrey's SUV and started the short drive to Hampton.

"Audrey, do you still have Michael's Saab Sonett?"

"Oh yes. He made me promise to keep it for Su, so it sits in our garage. I drive it now and again. It's a real odd car but it seems like it's a promise that I should keep."

"I would like to see it sometime."

"Sure, maybe you would like to take it for a drive?"

"That would be cool."

"So James, when do you fly out to Newport, Rhode Island?"

"Two days from now."

"Too bad you aren't going to stay."

"I'll be back next week. It was hard to pass up a trip to Newport, Rhode Island, and an Annapolis boat show."

"I'm sure you'll have a great time."

Audrey's home was a beautiful, early 1900s mini mansion that overlooked the Hampton harbor. The home was originally owned by Michael's grandparents and was repurchased by Audrey from its current owners two years after Michael's death. Audrey had restored it to its 1900s' splendor as a tribute to the Kenney family.

"Down the street is the Hampton Yacht Club where Michael and generations of Kenneys sailed. In fact, Michael's father Stephen Kenny was quite a sailing legend. I'll take you there and show you all the trophies belonging to the Kenney family. Maybe we can get one of the club boats and take a sail on the bay."

"I would really like that."

Audrey and Su's bedrooms were on the first floor, with four other bedrooms on the second floor.

"I suggest the girls sleep together in Su's room," Audrey announced.

"Mommy, can I?"

"Sure."

"Jade, you and James can take the large bedroom at the top of the stairs."

"Okay, great."

"Let me walk you up there and show you around."

The room was huge and really kind of spooky. I wondered how comfortable I would be when James left for his trip.

"Why don't you and James settle in? Take a shower if you like and freshen up. I'll prepare some snacks and drinks and we can meet on the back porch in an hour or so."

"Okay, great. I think I'll lie down for a half-hour."

"Take your time. I'm sure you must be exhausted from the trip." Audrey walked down the long winding stairway and vanished.

"So James, this is where it all started."

"I guess so."

"I think we need to go over to the cemetery sometime and visit Michael's grave."

"Don't be so dark. Let's enjoy the moment. I think that the tub is made for two."

"James, we are not having sex in Michael's house."

"Why not?"

"I don't know, you pervert." Suddenly there was a knock on the door. It was Audrey.

"I decided that maybe you need some help with your wind-down, so this is for you." She handed me a silver tray that included two glasses, a bottle of wine and some fresh fruit. At that moment, I knew James would have his way with me.

Chapter 29

The Drawing

An hour later, James and I made our way down to the porch where Audrey was sipping a glass of red wine.

"Well, you look very refreshed."

"Yes, we feel much better. That bedroom and bath are very nice."

Audrey took a deep breath. "I love that room. It is so romantic. Sometimes I go up to that room and lie on the bed and wish Michael was here."

"The ceiling fan is really unusual. Where did you get it?"

"It was in the old apartment where Michael lived."

"Oh I remember. It was discussed in his journal."

"Yes, that is the fan that he used to stare at and where his obsession was born. I sometimes think that it was the single element in his life that kept us apart for so many years."

"So where are the girls?"

"They're in the backyard playing on the tree swing."

"That's interesting. We have a tree swing, too."

"Well, we never had one before the girls started talking. Su wanted one like Ruby's so I had a handyman from the neighborhood construct one."

"I think the girls really hit it off."

"Yes, I agree. Oh, by the way, Mickey Dermott is in town, though he has to fly back to France tomorrow. He said he may stop by for a drink. He would love to see you."

"That's great. It's been a long time since I saw him last."

"You'll be surprised; he has aged quite a bit in the last five years."

"Why? Is there anything wrong?"

"No, I don't think so. He just seems so stressed out all the time."

James interrupted the conversation. "I think I'll go outside and check on the girls. Would you excuse me?"

"Sure, have fun. So tell me more about Mickey."

"Well, he seemed to change when Michael died. Then when Michael's adopted parents died, it really affected him. And I don't think all this travel is helping either."

"That's a shame."

Our conversation was interrupted by the doorbell. "That's probably Mickey."

"Jade, how are you?" Mickey announced as he walked onto the porch.

"Mickey, so nice to see you."

"I don't have much time. I'm sure Audrey told you I have a flight to Nice tomorrow but I wanted to stop by and see you. Jade, you look great."

"Thanks; you too."

"No need to fib. I've had a rough time over the past few years."

"I filled her in," Audrey said.

"So, where's James?"

"He's outside with the girls."

"I must go see him and I want to see Ruby."

"Mickey, I need some legal advice. Can we talk?"

"Sure, let me go outside and say hello to everyone and then I'll be back."

"Jade, is everything okay with the business?" asked Audrey.

"Yes, everything is going fine there. I need some other legal assistance. I'll explain when Mickey returns." A few minutes later, Mickey and James returned to the porch.

"Jade, that's quite a little girl you have there. She is really special."

"Thanks, Mickey."

"So what can I do for you?"

"I remember from reading in Michael's journal that you had done some investigation work for him. Didn't he hire you to find Jost, Sonnet and Audrey?"

"Yes, I did that work as a special favor."

"Well, I need one more favor."

"What do you need, Jade?"

"I'm trying to find anything and everything about a man named John Lyr. He lives in Albany, New York, and is a U.S. citizen. I have his address but not much else."

"Why do you need this information?"

"I have a hunch he knows something that I need to know."

"Okay, tell me more."

"I really don't know anything else."

"Okay, let me look into it and I'll call you in a few weeks."

"Great. Thanks so much."

"Glad to help. Look, I have to get going. I'll be in touch. It was great to see you."

"Mickey, have a safe trip to Nice and thanks."

We hugged each other and Mickey departed. Moments later, the girls walked in.

"Mom, can Ruby and I play in my room?"

"Sure."

"Do you want to see my room?" asked Su.

"We would love to."

Su's room looked like typical eleven-year-old's room except that Audrey had gone to great lengths to include many pictures of Michael.

"May I see the pictures of your father?"

Su handed me a stack of pictures that Audrey had accumulated from Michael's parents. There were a few that were taken at the end of his life and I was shocked to see how fast he had aged at the end.

"Su, show Jade and James some of the pictures you recently drew."

Su went into the closet and took out a dozen or so pictures.

"Show them the latest one." Su thumbed through the stack and pulled out a large drawing. She held it up for us to see, but she didn't expect to see the shocked look on our faces. Audrey recognized our discomfort but decided not to probe us in front of the girls.

"Wow, Su, you sure are talented. That's a great picture," James said in a very guarded way.

"Do you want to see the others?"

"Sure, I'd love to."

"Well, here's a picture of my dad, and here's a picture of my mom, and here's a picture of Ruby."

I picked up the pictures and studied them. They were really well done and very accurate but the picture of Ruby was when she was much younger and way before the girls were talking. "Su, I'm curious—how do you know what Ruby looked like back then?"

"I don't remember but I probably dreamt it. A lot of my pictures come to me in my dreams."

"Is that where the picture of that man came from?"

"Well kind of, I think."

Audrey could tell that I was really fixated on the first picture. "Let me ask you. Who is the man in that picture?"

"I don't know; just some person."

"Did you dream about him?"

"Yes, I first saw a picture of him in a magazine."

"Really. What magazine?"

Su walked over to another stack of papers that were sitting on her desk. She sorted through the pile and pulled out a single page which had been ripped out of a magazine. She handed it to me. It was a picture of John. The footer on the page said The Wine Guide and was dated August of last year. I could tell that the picture was from an ad rather than an article, so any hope of learning more about John was not likely. I handed it to James, who took a quick glance at it.

"Yep, that's him."

Then Ruby looked at the picture.

"Mommy, that's him, that's the creepy man from the airport."

"Ruby, calm down."

"Mommy, that's too weird."

"Yes, I know."

Audrey spoke up, "Jade, what's going on? How do you know this guy?"

"Audrey, buckle your seat belt; the roller coaster is about to depart."

Chapter 30

Lyr, Lyr, Pants on Fire

Su began to put away her pictures and little else was said about John, as neither James nor I wanted to disclose all the details of our encounters with John in front of the girls.

"Let's go back to the porch. There is a bottle of cab waiting for us."

"Good idea."

The girls continued to play in Su's room, which was convenient, as it was clear that Audrey wanted the full lowdown on John.

"Okay, Jade. I'm buckled in."

"First off, that is the guy I asked Mickey to research. We met on the plane yesterday."

"How did you meet him?"

"He kept staring at Ruby. Then he sat next to me for a few minutes and asked me if we had met before."

"Had you?"

"No, I never saw him before, though I did have two dreams about him later on."

James looked over at me but said nothing. "I got his name from his immigration form and then did some research on the Internet."

"What did you find?"

"Nothing, though he did tell me he had some ownership in the vineyard in Franschhoek."

"Where is Franschhoek?"

"It's about sixty miles east of Cape Town."

"Do you know what vineyard?"

"No, but I can take a guess."

"Okay, tell me."

"M.S. Vineyard."

"Why do you think so?"

"Just a wild guess. When I left Frankfurt, I ordered a single serving bottle of wine from the flight attendant. The bottle was from M.S. Vineyards, Franschhoek. Given how weird and coincidental everything has been and recognizing the power of Michael and all we just experienced with Su's picture, it's a good bet John Lyr is associated with M.S. Vineyards."

"Very interesting. I'll be right back."

Audrey left the room, leaving James and me alone to fact-check each other. "What do you think Audrey's doing?" I asked.

"No idea, but you are the one that said this would be a roller coaster ride."

Audrey returned, carrying a large book. "This book was published about ten years ago. It's a grape growers and wine producers guide. They no longer publish it; the Internet probably killed off the publisher." Audrey paged to the South Africa section and then started searching. The vineyards were first listed by country, then alphabetically by vineyard name. "Here it is, M.S. Vineyards. Let me see … established 1971, produces mostly reds, just over 500,000 bottles annually, most wine ranked in the high 80s or 90s, export limited to Europe, located in Franschhoek, owner is M.S. Industries Ltd. There is no reference to John Lyr."

"Can I see that?"

Audrey handed me the book. I glanced over the text but all the information was very unrevealing. "I wonder why John appeared in the advertisement for the South African Growers Association?"

"Jade, that's a very good question."

"I wonder if we should chase that rabbit down the hole. Better yet, I think I will email Mickey Dermott to let him know what we have found. I want to make sure he fully researches M.S. Vineyards. Audrey, there is one other thing about John. He owns a vintage Saab Sonett."

"You must be kidding. Okay, I am really buying into this coincidence theory of yours."

"And one other thing, he says he's not married. In fact, he said he never was married but yet, he is wearing a wedding ring. He is hiding something. I'm 99 percent sure."

"Well, if he is hiding something, Mickey will find it. James, you have been pretty quiet. What do you think?"

"I was hoping you weren't going to ask. I had to laugh when Jade made mention of the roller coaster ride because that is what the last several years have felt like. Every emotion you can think of I have felt, including regrets. At times our marriage has suffered and for a while, the Ruby/Michael issue was all we talked about. That made me retreat to the marina where I could put my head into something other than Michael Kenney. Please don't think I'm not grateful for the gift he gave us. The marina in Cape Town is our livelihood and we are very happy owning and operating it. But because he willed it to Jade, I feel a certain obligation to support her, and now you, on his quest for understanding. It is particularly difficult for me to embrace all this because I'm such a black-and-white kind of person. All this spirituality doesn't come natural to me. So there is a long-winded answer to what was a simple question."

Audrey sighed. "Michael has given all of us such wonderful things but there's a price that seems to go along with it."

"Yes I agree, but I think we are close to realizing paid in full."

Chapter 31

Mixed Emotions

James began to show mixed emotions about his upcoming trip to Newport and Annapolis. I wasn't sure why, but I had convinced myself that there were only two possibilities. One, he felt that we were approaching a breakthrough in the whole Michael Kenney saga and he wanted to stay engaged in the final process; or two, he was so enamored with Audrey that he wanted to see more of her. I had tried to suppress my feelings of jealousy, but unfortunately, was not successful. James could sense it and tried to pry open my feelings, but I couldn't tell him.

When sunrise came, we quietly slipped out of the house and started our short ride to the Newport News airport. Audrey had encouraged us to use the Saab but we instead elected for the more modern SUV. The ride to the airport was uneventful and James and I talked mostly about his trip, when he would be calling and when he would be picked up at the airport. I decided to park the SUV and walked into the airport with him. We had a quick cup of coffee, rehashed the same discussion we had on the ride over and then said goodbye. As James moved toward the security area, he gave me the obligatory kiss and the obligatory "I love you" and walked away. And for a moment, it felt like he was walking out of my life forever. I stood there and watched him until he was no longer in view and then proceeded back to the truck, feeling fairly depressed.

When I arrived back at the house everyone was still sleeping. I stood at the kitchen window looking out at Sunset Creek and at the note left by Audrey; "Take the Saab." The keys were lying next to the note. "What the hell," I said to myself. The Saab was housed in a detached garage beside the mini-mansion. I opened the garage door and walked in. I slid my hand over the roof. "So Michael, what great secret will I discover today?" I opened the door, sat down, put the key into the ignition, and took a deep breath. The Saab had a strange but pleasant smell, a combination of ginger and orange. I attributed it to the new leather seats and carpet that had just been installed as part of Audrey's restoration effort.

I turned the key and in a few seconds, the engine started. The engine whined like a two-cycle motorcycle engine and then relaxed into a gentle purr. I shifted into reverse, backed out of the driveway and began driving to who knows where. "Cool car," I said to myself. "Su is really going to like it when it becomes hers."

I drove for ten minutes, not knowing where I was

going and not really keeping track of my right and left turns. It didn't really seem important to me that I didn't know exactly how to get back to Audrey's, but somehow I assumed I would figure it out. I wandered for a few minutes and finally realized where I was. I stopped the Saab, got out and walked until I got to my destination. I closed my eyes and began to recount that day many years ago when I stood at Michael's grave. It was the day that Paul Curry gave me the letter and the day I realized that somehow Ruby and Michael would be connected. Then I opened my eyes and looked down at his headstone. "So Michael, here I am. What do you want to tell me? What's next? What should I do now?" A weird feeling came over me, as if I had been given the answer to these questions. The answer was simple. Drive. I walked back to the Saab, got in and started to drive; to where, I didn't know.

I drove through Buckroe and other parts of Hampton until I saw a sign that read Grandview. I pulled over to the side of the road and tried to remember why this name seemed so familiar. Then it hit me. There were several references to this place in Michael's journal. I recalled that this was where he would drive during some of his troubling times so he could think and meditate. It was also where Jost and Sonnet, his pre-incarnate and pre-incarnate sister, had drifted in a small sailboat and where they had spent a cold lonely night.

I continued to drive. At the end of Grandview was a small beach that looked out onto the bay. I turned in to a small parking lot, shut off the engine and started to stare at the beams of light that were created by the rising sunlight reflected on the light chop. "Michael, talk to me. What am I doing here? What is the significance of John, La Teek, and Dr. Blink? How are they all related and are we near the end of our journey?" These questions were not to be answered but I knew these were the correct questions to be asking.

I closed my eyes and tried to force myself into a dreamlike state. I was successful. A voice appeared in my head, "Laura, I love you. Laura, I love you." The voice was familiar but I couldn't place it and for a second, I thought it might be Blink's voice. Then I heard the voice again and again. "Who is that voice?" I thought.

Then another voice entered my head. "Man, I love you." This voice was a female and sounded like no one I had ever heard before. It was clearly a new voice. I continued to focus back on the first voice. "Say it again," I said aloud, but no voice replied.

Then it hit me. It was John's voice somewhat disguised behind crying. It was John and I was sure of it.

Then a small black and brown towhee landed on the hood of the Saab and began tapping on the windshield. Though the tapping was gentle, it was enough to wake me from my dream. This was a sign that it was time to retrace my steps back to Audrey's house.

Chapter 32

Who is Man?

I arrived at the house at ten o'clock and it was clear from the level of activity that was going on that I had missed a few of the daily rituals. Audrey was washing the breakfast dishes and the girls and Audrey were showered and dressed.

"Mommy, where have you been?"

"I decided to go for a short drive."

"Short drive—you've been gone for two hours!"

"Has it been that long?"

"Where did you go?"Audrey asked.

"I drove over to Phoebus and then to Grandview."

"Did you stop by the cemetery?"

"Yes."

"Did you have any revelations?"

"No, but I did drive to Grandview and parked the car for a while. Then I fell asleep for a few minutes. I had some very interesting dreams."

"What did you dream?"

"I'll tell you in a minute." I left the kitchen and walked upstairs to the guest room. Then I retrieved the tiles that La Teek had given me and returned to the kitchen. Once there, I opened the leather pouch and dumped the tiles onto the kitchen table. Next I turned the tiles letter up and began to place them in alphabetical order. Audrey walked over to the table.

"Jade, what's going on?"

"These are the tiles I had gotten from that woman I told you about—La Teek. She told me that these tiles will guide me to the answer."

"Yes, I know you mentioned that before. So what are you trying to spell?"

"Laura and Man."

"Why those names?"

"They came to me when I was sitting in the car at Grandview."

"Okay, let's see what we can spell."

Laura was a bust as there was no L, U, or R. "Man," on the other hand, was represented in the tiles.

"What do you suppose Man means?" asked Audrey.

"I don't know. Maybe it's part of a name like Manfred, Manny or Mandela, or maybe it's a reference to Mandala, the origin of the sand from Michael's journal." I reached into my pocket and took out a small piece of paper and wrote the name Man on it and then put it into the pouch along with the tiles. Then I told Audrey all the details surrounding the visit from La Teek as well as a reference made to her in Dr. Blink's journal.

"Audrey, may I use the computer?"

"Of course."

"I want to send Mickey Dermott an email letting him know that in his search for John he should also consider the name Laura, as I think they may be connected."

Audrey's computer was fairly new and booted up quickly. I quickly shot an email to Mickey and then decided to check my email account at Mac Delivery Service. There were about forty emails; the usual junk mail took up half of the email volume. There were others from slip renters and then one that really perked my interest. The subject section read, "I would like to see the Swan." I opened the email. It was from John.

> *James,*
>
> *I hope your journey to Virginia and beyond is going well. I looked at your website this morning and noticed your brokerage listing. The Swan looks very nice but maybe a bit too large. How can I get some more specifics about the boat? I will be back in South Africa next month and would like to see it, assuming you haven't sold it. How negotiable is the price? You mentioned that it was owned by an estate. Do you know if the estate has been settled or who I have to deal with? What is the name of the estate trustee? Email me back when you have a chance and send my regards to Jade and Ruby.*
>
> *John.*

I took note of John's email address which clearly indicated that it was a U.S.-based email account. "Hey Audrey, come check this out."

Audrey reviewed the email.

"Wow, that was quick."

"I guess he's hot to buy a boat or maybe the boat is just an excuse for him to see Ruby and me. Only time will tell."

"Jade, regarding your tiles, I noticed that there was an "S," as in M & S Vineyards."

"Yes, that's occurred to me as well. I'll make a note of it and add it to the piece of paper that I put into the pouch. So what's on the agenda for today?"

"Well, I thought we would go to the yacht club for lunch and then depending on the winds, maybe we could take the girls out for short sail."

"That sounds like fun."

"Su has been taking sailing lessons for the last couple of years and is a pretty good little sailor. The yacht club is holding a nice 18-foot daysailer which would be perfect for this afternoon."

"Great. Sounds like a plan."

By 12:30, we were on our way for the short walk to the yacht club and a trip down memory lane.

Chapter 33

An Uncomfortable Conversation

The yacht club seemed to be a happy place full of mid-lifers and blue hairs all there to dine in the presence of the fleet. The club catered mostly to puffers, a South African term for sailor, especially those who were of the racing type. The club had been known throughout the area for having produced excellent race teams. Michael's father, Stephen Kenney, and Michael's supposed pre-incarnate Jost Alexson, were some of the most revered.

At the bar stood an old man who greeted Audrey with a kind of fondness for which I was not particularly accustomed. I leaned over to Audrey. "Is that Jackie Vee?"

"Yes, quite an interesting guy. He's about ninety-five years old."

"Wow!"

"He is a real fixture around here."

The girls walked over to an empty table and sat down. It was abundantly clear that Su and Audrey were regulars. A young teenage waitress walked over to the table.

"Hi, Su. Hello, Mrs. Kenney."

"Hello, Helen."

"Will it be four or five?"

"Four plus the usual."

"What's that all about?" I asked.

"Su likes to have a place setting for Michael. I know it's weird but it's sort of tradition, and the entire wait staff knows about it. It used to bother me but I just let Su have her way. She only does it at the yacht club, never at home or anywhere else."

Lunch was quite enjoyable and I wondered how a restaurant would do at our marina in Cape Town. After lunch we walked down to the end of a dock and boarded a Rhodes 19. The Rhodes was fitted with a small outboard engine and what looked like a new mainsail and headsail. Su boarded the boat like she did it every day and started the engine. Audrey handed out life jackets while I managed the dock lines.

"Are we ready?" Audrey asked.

"Full steam ahead!" Ruby shouted.

Su helmed the boat out of the marina and into the mouth of the Hampton River. Minutes later the mainsail was raised and the engine shut off. The winds were steady at ten knots, perfect for a Rhodes 19. Everyone seemed very focused on sailing until the questions started. Ruby started in.

"Mommy, are Su and I sisters?"

"No, of course not."

"Well, we think we are."

"You can't be; you have different fathers."

"We think Su's daddy is my daddy, too."

"No, that's not possible."

"Then why did Su's daddy try to talk to me and why did you have me going to Dr. Blink?"

"Enough questions. Let's focus on sailing."

"Are you and daddy going to get a divorce?"

"Of course not. Stop with the questions."

"Why are you and daddy fighting?"

"We're not fighting; stop with the questions."

"Mommy, do you love John?"

"Ruby, enough!"

Audrey remained silent for quite awhile and then spoke up. "Ruby, why don't you take the helm? Su, show Ruby how to steer."

"I don't want to steer. I want answers!"

"Ruby, everything is fine with your father and I don't even know John."

"Well, you seem very interested in him like you were in Su's daddy. Is Daddy coming back?"

"Yes. Now stop with the questions and let's focus on sailing."

Then Su started in. "Ruby and I have been talking and we think that John may be okay."

"Why did you come to that conclusion?"

"He has a nice smile and I think he was once very sad."

"Why?"

"He lost his wife like I lost my father."

"How do you know he had a wife?"

"Ruby and I have compared our dreams over the last few nights and we both dreamt about John."

"What did you dream?"

"I saw him at a funeral. He was crying and saying something about the person who died."

"What did he say?"

"Laura, I love you."

"What did you say?"

"I think he said, 'Laura, I love you'."

"Are you sure?"

"Well, Ruby and I talked about it and that's what we came up with."

Audrey looked over at me and raised one eyebrow. "So what else do you two know about John?"

"Nothing. That's it."

"Okay, can we change the subject?"

Ruby and Su looked at each other and agreed to stop the interrogation. Over the next few hours, we took turns at the helm and trimming the sails. I was pleasantly surprised how well we worked as a team and how well the boat sailed. Sometimes I felt like restarting the conversation about John, as I was starting to feel that semi-obsession, uncontrollable feeling that I once had about Michael. But Ruby was already so paranoid about James and our relationship that I didn't want to make her feel any more insecure.

Chapter 34

L. Y. R.

At eight in the morning on the sixth day of our vacation, I received a call from James. He told me all about his conference and the races in Newport. I could detect a real spunkiness in his voice and whatever had gotten in the way of our relationship had resolved itself. Just before he hung up he told me that he had bought a special gift for me and was anxious to get to Annapolis so he could then get back to see Ruby et al. I handed the phone to Ruby and after a few minutes, she ended the call with an "I love you Daddy soooooo much."

I had been checking email for something from Mickey but no emails were to be found. I had taken a few rides in the Saab by myself and even went back to Grandview but no new revelations occurred. However, this was not the case for Su and Ruby. Each night a little more information was revealed to them as they dreamed. But for their own reasons they had not wanted to share all that they had learned.

The picture of John that Su had drawn was now hanging on her wall and no longer was Ruby speaking negatively about him. Several days later, while having breakfast, Su decided to open up.

"I think we know more about John."

"What do you know and how did you find out the information?"

"I've been dreaming about him and his family."

"What do you mean, family?"

Su took out a piece of paper that was folded in thirds and unfolded it. She then flattened it and slid it over to me. There were three words written on it. One of the words was familiar to me.

"What is this?" I asked.

"These are the names I have been hearing in my dreams. Ruby has also been hearing the same names."

"Do you know what they mean?"

"I think they have something to do with the man I drew the picture of, the guy in the wine magazine; you know, John."

I pushed the paper over to Audrey: Laura, Yanna, Rose. "It looks like John's initials."

"What do you mean?" I asked.

"You said his last name was Lyr; Laura, Yanna, Rose."

"I hadn't noticed that."

I excused myself from the table and walked to the bedroom and retrieved the tiles and returned to the kitchen. I pulled out a piece of paper and looked at the words that I had written down: Man and Laura.

Then I wrote the two other names on a sticky note and placed it in the pouch.

"Mommy, can I see the pouch?"

"Sure."

Ruby spilled the tiles onto the table and started to arrange the tiles but the only name that could be spelled was MAN.

"I think I need to email Mickey," I said and walked over to Audrey's computer.

Mickey,

I hope all is well in Nice. As you do your research on John Lyr, please consider the following names: Man, Laura, Yanna, Rose. These names could be related to his family, maybe his wife and kids' names. I think he is or was married and has or had two children. have no clue about the name Man, but maybe it's a nickname for Manfred or Manson or something like that. I look forward to your return email. Stay well and take care of yourself.

Jade.

I walked back to the table and re-engaged in the discussion with Su and Ruby. "Is there anything else you have noticed when you are dreaming about him?"

"What do you mean?"

"Well, what type of setting was he in, in the dream? Was he in a city, or in the country, in the mountains or near the water, or anything like that?"

Ruby and Su looked at each other as if they were searching for something to say but nothing was forthcoming. After the breakfast dishes were done, Audrey and I walked to the rear porch. The girls remained inside the house.

"So Audrey, what do you make of all this?"

"I don't know. The whole thing is very intriguing. It really makes me want to meet this mystery man."

"Do you suppose he has something to do with the replacement?"

"I don't know, but the idea has crossed my mind."

"Are you attracted to him?"

She paused for a second. "Don't be silly. How can you be attracted to a picture?"

"Well, he is a little more than a picture, so let me ask you again. Are you attracted to him?"

"Sort of."

We both laughed and decided to drop the subject. Just then, the phone rang. It was James. He had called to check in and to let us know that he would be arriving at the airport at four o'clock as scheduled. I confirmed that we would be there to pick him up. We exchanged a few more sentences, mainly about Ruby, and then terminated the call.

Chapter 35

Third Party Confirmation

Seeing James walk through the terminal was a welcome sight. He looked very refreshed and wind burned and had a real snap in his step. He was carrying a bouquet of flowers and a shopping bag that looked to be holding wrapped presents.

"Hello, ladies," he said as he handed the flowers to Audrey.

"Thank you, James. You're so sweet."

"Thanks. Jade, your gift is in the bag."

"I can hardly wait. So how was your flight?"

"It was very short from Baltimore to Newport News. Just forty-five minutes."

"So how was the boat show?" asked Audrey.

"Terrific. Jade, you would have loved it."

"So what's new with Ruby and Su?"

"Not too much. They are inseparable and really

have had a great time with each other."

"Have you heard from Mickey yet?"

"No, but I have had a few more data points."

"Really?"

"Yes, but I'll fill you in later when we get back to the house."

"Where are the girls?"

"They are at the yacht club. They have a sailing class. We'll pick them up on the way back to the house."

"Great. I can't wait to see them."

As evening approached, we found ourselves back on the porch enjoying a glass of wine. I was beginning to worry about our departure which was now only three days away. I had concerns about how Ruby and Su would handle their separation and wondered if either would relapse back into their old problems.

James had carried the three presents down to the porch and presented me with a small box. I opened it and gazed at the beautiful necklace.

"James, it's beautiful."

"Thanks, I got it in Newport. It's a spinel crystal that is cut to match the lens cut of the Newport Lighthouse."

"Put it on me."

James came behind me and secured the clasp.

"Wow, Jade, that looks great on you," announced Audrey.

"James, I love it."

"By the way, I have another gift."

"Really, what?"

"Information. When I was in Annapolis I met a

guy who works for the intelligence industry. I told him about John Lyr and he said he would take a look into the situation. Just before I got on the plane, he texted me to tell me that John Lyr is a dually."

"Really?"

Audrey interrupted, "What is a dually?"

"Oh, it's a slang term for someone who has dual citizenship or someone who carries a passport from another country. Like me. You see, my father was born in Scotland and I was born in South Africa. Because my father is a citizen of the UK, I could elect to either have a South African or British passport. I elected British because it's a lot easier to travel in Europe with the UK passport than a South African passport."

"Very interesting," Audrey said.

"So James, what is his dual citizenship?"

"He is American and Canadian."

"That's weird. I really need to tell Mickey about this. Did you find out anything else?"

"No, but this guy told me that if he found out anything else he would let me know."

"What is his name?"

"Okay, ready for this? James," he paused, "Bond." We all laughed. Minutes later, I was back on the Internet emailing Mickey the latest bit of information. Then I rejoined James and Audrey and filled James in on what I had learned from Ruby and Su. He seemed intrigued by the whole thing and asked if I was able to spell any of the names with the tiles. I told him the only word that worked was "man." We both agreed that being able to spell "man" out of all the letters was of no consequence.

Minutes later, James's phone rang. He glanced at the name with a puzzled look and said, "It's Bond, James Bond."

"Hello, Mr. Bond. This is a surprise."

"How was your flight back to Newport News?"

"Good, thanks."

"Listen, I have done a little bit more digging on your Mr. Lyr."

"Great. Can I put you on speakerphone so my wife can listen in?"

"Sure."

"So what did you find out?"

"The passport that Mr. Lyr holds was issued five years ago."

"So is that a problem?"

"Yes, it was not a renewal."

"What do you mean?"

I mean he never had a passport before, yet I remember you telling me that he owned a vineyard in South Africa for many years and I just thought that if a U.S. citizen had been traveling to South Africa, he would have had a passport. But the records I was able to review showed no renewal. It's like this guy just appeared on Earth five years ago and started anew."

"Is there any chance that maybe he changed his name?"

"No, that would normally show up in the passport renewal records unless he never had a passport under a previous name."

"Well, thanks for the info."

"I thought you'd want to know."

"Yes, definitely. Thank you, Mr. Bond," I said with

deliberate emphasis.

"My pleasure. I'll see you next month."

"Sure thing. Goodbye."

"James, what's that about?"

"He's coming to Cape Town to look at a boat that is being built for him. He is thinking about putting it in our marina for a while before he sails it home."

"What's he buying?"

"A Leopard 434."

"Nice boat."

Chapter 36

A Sad Goodbye

Some goodbyes you look forward to and some you don't. This goodbye was bittersweet. On one hand, I didn't want to leave because I was having such a good time and the girls never seemed happier. I was also making progress on my quest to unlock the John mystery. On the other hand, I was feeling just a slight bit jealous over how enamored James was with Audrey. I would have been even more concerned if Audrey seemed especially enamored by James, but she didn't seem to be.

We had decided that Audrey and Su would make a visit to South Africa around Christmas time, which was only three months away. That seemed to allay the concerns I had about the girls saying goodbye.

I wanted James to drive the Sonett before we left, so on the morning of our evening departure, we headed out for a quick spin in Michael Kenney's Saab Sonett.

James started the V-4 engine and backed out of the driveway.

"So Jade, where to?"

"Let's go where the car wants to go." He raised his eyebrows and looked at me as if I had gone insane. Strangely enough, we ended up at the cemetery and then at Grandview. "James, why did you drive here?"

"I don't know, why?"

"This is where I ended up when I drove the car the first time." Then I instructed him to turn into the small parking lot that I had visited on my first drive. We sat there for a moment staring out at the Chesapeake Bay. Then James leaned over and kissed me. The kiss was long and deep and I could feel sudden arousal. He slid his hand onto my thigh and started to move to my area of arousal, but then stopped.

"Jade, did you hear that?"

I hesitated to say yes, so instead I said, "Hear what?

"Did you just hear someone say Laura?"

I took a deep breath. "Yes, I heard it and I heard it before at this place."

Then I gripped his head and brought it back to my lips. The kiss continued, but again was interrupted by "Laura, I love you." Only this time James didn't hear it because it was he who had said it.

"James, stop joking."

"I didn't say anything."

"Yes, you did. You said, 'Laura, I love you'."

"No, I didn't." But at that moment, I realized that James was in a fog and had no idea what was coming out of his mouth. He said it again, but this time in a more anguished tone.

"James, let's get out of here." But he didn't move. "James!" He didn't reply. "James!" There was still no reply. Then out of desperation, I slapped him across the face.

He jumped back. "Hey, what was that for?"

"Let's get out of here." James backed out and drove out of the parking lot.

"Jade, what just happened?"

"I think you just had a little taste of Michael Kenney."

"I wonder if that's what happens to Ruby?"

"Who knows?"

"So you think Michael just got into my head? Maybe there is a connection between Michael, John and Laura."

"Do you think somehow Michael's soul and John's soul are connected?"

"I wouldn't be surprised."

"But how would we find out?"

"James, I think we need to assume so."

"Okay, I will make the leap."

Very little was said again until we pulled into the driveway of Audrey's house.

"James, let's not say anything about what just happened."

"Why?"

"I don't want to revisit it right now."

I was very surprised that there were no tears shed during our goodbyes. The girls had agreed to email each other as soon as we got to the UK, assuming we had computer access at James's parents' country home.

The flight to JFK was uneventful. The flight to Gatwick was delayed two hours due to air traffic in the New York metro area. We finally departed New York close to midnight. James and I had decided to take a sleeping pill, to help cope with the long flight. Minutes later, we were all in a deep sleep. The next thing I remembered was the sound of the pilots saying that we were on our initial approach into Gatwick and that he apologized for the delay in New York. As we touched down, James, Ruby and I compared notes and were grateful for seven hours of dreamless sleep.

Chapter 37

Seven Hundred Years Ago

The village of Houghton, West Sussex, was home to forty-nine fine British citizens. The village also was the home to three taverns, one of which had the notoriety of being the second-oldest continually operated pub in all of England. The village was once part of the estate of the Duke of Norfolk. The houses and the buildings were sold off in the 1950s to the general public and James's great aunt was fortunate enough to have acquired two small cottages which she had combined into a single house. According to West Sussex records, the cottages dated back to the 1200s. The house, named Little Wyndham, was the summer home to James's family and to the legendary ghosts that would appear in the kitchen pantry area and in the upstairs guest room.

This was Ruby's first trip to the UK and her excitement was uncontrollable. She asked question after question about the houses, people, countryside, thatched roofs, castles and other historic buildings. By the time we completed our forty-five minute trip to Houghton, she had worn me out. We planned to stay there for a few days on our own and then would be joined by James's immediate family. As we unlocked the vestibule door, I could recall the essence of the house. I remembered the creak of the door and the semi-musty smell that seven hundred-year-old homes produce. There were fresh flowers on the dining room table that had been placed there by the caretaker. There was coal in the fireplace and two bottles of wine parked on the counter near the pantry. James and I unpacked and took a quick shower. Then he and Ruby went off to Pullborough to buy some groceries. I intentionally decided to stay behind, despite urging from James and Ruby to come along. But I had a hidden agenda and my opportunity to fulfill it was very limited.

I walked to the kitchen and closed the swinging door behind me. I lowered the shades to create as much darkness as possible. Then I sat down on the floor beside the pantry and closed my eyes.

"Michael, I want to talk to you. Michael, Man, Laura, Yanna, Rose. Someone talk to me, please!"

I sat there in silence, waiting for something to happen. I could feel the cold temperature of the floor through my pants, but at the same time, I could feel beads of sweat forming on my forehead. I confirmed the sensation and pondered its oddity.

Then I began to hear a voice in the distance. It sounded like it was coming from inside my head. I listened again. The voice was familiar to me. I concentrated on it. "Michael, is that you?"

The voice got louder and now I could hear it more clearly. The voice was slowly singing one word, "Laura, Laura."

"Michael, why are you singing this? Michael, tell me, please."

I could now feel a cool breeze on my back but my forehead was still dripping with sweat. I raised my hand and touched my forehead and realized it was on fire. My thought process was scrambling. "I must have a fever or something," I thought to myself.

"Michael, are you doing this to me? Please stop."

"Look inside, just look inside."

The pantry door opened slightly. But I refused to open it.

Michael's voice grew louder, "Open the door."

But I was too afraid.

"Jade, open the door, open the door." But this time it wasn't Michael's voice. It was James. I got up and looked at my watch. An hour had elapsed. I got up and walked toward the vestibule. James and Ruby were standing there with their arms full of groceries. I checked my forehead. It was cool and dry. James put the groceries on the table.

"I'll put them away."

"Okay."

"Why don't you and Ruby take a walk down the Bury Road and look at the farm animals?"

"Ruby, do you want to do that?"

"Sure, Daddy."

Minutes later, I was again alone in the kitchen. I immediately brightened the room by returning the shades to the open position. Then I started to put away all the groceries that required refrigerating until I was forced to face the pantry. I stood there staring at it, afraid of it. Then I reached for the door handle. It was hot, as if there was a fire burning on the other side of the door. I opened the door slowly and could detect a strong burnt smell, the kind that comes from a well-used fireplace. It overwhelmed me for a second. I decided the smell was too strong and that it needed to be aired out, so I opened the door wide and opened the window. Then something caught my eye and every ounce of air was taken from my lungs. On the inside of the door were soot lines. I looked at them and touched them. The door was hot and the soot marks were fresh. I recognized the word formed by the soot lines. There were just three letters. M A N.

Later that evening James, Ruby, and I sat in the living room trying to unwind. There was an odd silence that came over the room which was not typical, given that Ruby was there. I had decided not to say anything about my experience earlier in the day as I didn't want to make Ruby uncomfortable or James angry. I needed to break the silence. "So, Ruby, what you think of this old house?"

"I like it."

"What do you like about it?"

"I feel like my friends are here."

James shot me an uncomfortable glance.

"Has there ever been a fire in this house?" Ruby asked.

I shifted my position in the chair and James immediately knew I was outside my comfort zone. "You probably smell the old fireplace."

"No, not that smell. This smells fresh like a fire just happened."

James entered the conversation. "I don't smell anything."

"Neither do I, Ruby. I'm sure it's the downdraft of the fireplace."

Ruby dropped the subject. "Come on, Ruby, it's bedtime."

James turned out the lights and we all walked upstairs. The upstairs of Little Wyndham was comprised of three bedrooms and two bathrooms. James and I took the master bedroom and Ruby took the larger of the two guest rooms. I helped her into her pajamas and showed her where the towels were kept. She washed her face and hands, brushed her teeth and went to bed. James and I did the same and then turned out the lights. I was taken by the darkness, stillness and silence.

I could tell by James' breathing that he had drifted off to sleep. I lay there for a long time thinking about the events of the day. I decided to check on Ruby, as I thought I could hear sounds coming from her room. The door was opened a crack and a small bit of light flashed into the room from a passing car. I could see Ruby sitting up in her bed. Her arms were gently swaying in the air. She was rocking back and forth as if she was summoning a spirit. Then another car passed by and another flash of light beamed into the room. A hundred shadows flashed before my eyes. I felt a slight grip on my neck and goose bumps grew on my arms. Ruby started to whisper.

"I'm glad you are all here. It's been a very long time."

Her arms were still waving and her body still rocking.

"Have you come to help me?" Ruby asked.

"Yes."

"Yes."

"Yes."

"Yes."

I was starting to panic as I heard the four distinct voices in my ear. I knew one of the voices.

"Michael, is that you?" Ruby asked.

"Just listen."

Another car passed by and the shadows appeared again. Then all of a sudden. Ruby started to speak and I realized who Ruby had summoned.

"Hello, Rose."

"Can I speak to Father now?"

"Yes Rose," Ruby replied.

"Father, we miss you. We want to come home."

Ruby's voice deepened to a man's voice.

"Rose, Yanna, I wish you could come home too, but you can't. I'm sorry."

"Can you come to us? Mother misses you."

"I miss her too," Ruby replied in John's voice. Then a new voice appeared.

"John, it's okay to move on. We will be there for you when it's your time."

Then Ruby quietly fell back on her bed, sighed and said, "Laura, I love you."

An immediate warm breeze blew across my neck and a gentle grip was released. I wandered back to bed and fell asleep several hours later.

I was awakened by this stream of sunlight that penetrated the crack between the edge of the shade and window casing. James had been up for a while as evidenced by the smell of fresh coffee. I walked into Ruby's room, noticing that she was in the middle of the awakening process. I sat on the edge of her bed.

"So Ruby, how did you sleep?"

"Great."

"Did you dream at all?"

"No, I don't think so."

"Are you sure you didn't dream about John and his family?"

"Oh that. I wasn't dreaming."

Chapter 38

Emails

The computer at the cottage was old but functional and it only took me a few attempts for the Internet to launch. Ruby was quick to email Su and then turned the keyboard over to me. There were about one hundred-fifty emails that had stacked up on the Mac Delivery Service server but only five really interested me. There was one from John, one from Paul Curry, one from Audrey, and two from Mickey Dermott. I opened Mickey's first.

Jade,

Thanks for your most recent email. I've not been able to find much about John Lyr though I did confirm everything you have found out from other sources. I have another contact from the credit bureau who is running a credit check to see if anything shows up. I will email you if I find out anything of interest.

The email ended with Mickey's typical salutation. Then I opened up his next email.

Jade,

Shortly after I sent the last email I heard from my contact. I was able to get some information about unusual expenditures that were made on his credit card over the last five years. There are only a few that were disclosed. One was an auto purchase for $30,000 in Albany, New York, at a VW dealership. There was a large block of airline tickets purchased from a British air-based travel agent for $25,000. And then there was a payment made to a private hospital in Moscow. This payment was for $51,000 and was made just before the issuance of his passport. So how he happened to have been in Moscow without a passport raises a lot of questions about this guy. I'm wondering if John Lyr is some sort of spy whose identity has been altered. I'll see what else I can find out but for now, that's all I could find. Stay well.

Mickey.

I thought about what Mickey said in his email and concluded that John was no spy. Spies don't leave immigration papers lying on their seat in an airplane.

Then I opened John's email.

Jade,

I hope you had a good visit with your friends. I am heading back to South Africa in a few days and want to make arrangements to see a few of the boats you are brokering. Please let me know when you'll be available. I look forward to hearing from you.

John.

Below his name was an auto signature. "John Lyr, M.S. Vineyards, Franschhoek, South Africa."

Next I opened Paul Curry's email.

Jade,

I hope this email finds you well. I understand from your office assistant that you are in the UK visiting James's family. I am also here and was wondering if you'd be able to get together for lunch. I'm about 100 km to the east, so perhaps we could meet halfway in Stenning. I also wanted to let you know that I spoke to Jodii the other day. He wanted me to tell you that you are on the right course. He said you are very close and that you should keep Audrey and Su close to you. I think he meant in the emotional and physical sense. He said you must peel away the layers, get under the veneer and seek the truth. The tiles hold the key. They spell out the answer. Jodii is working hard to help you figure this out. Please let me know if you can meet me for lunch.

Paul.

I replied immediately.

Paul,

It's so good to hear from you. I will check with James and get back to you. The info that follows are all the facts I have on the final piece of the puzzle. Please forward this email to Jodii. It may help him, help me.

I then disclosed everything I knew in exquisite detail and sent the email on to Paul. Then I opened the email from Audrey.

Jade,

We miss you, James and Ruby already and can't wait to see you in a few months. Su has become more and more interested in this John person. She has drawn two more pictures of him and she told me that she has been dreaming of him every night. The real strange thing is that I have also been thinking and dreaming about him as well. I have found myself frequently looking at his picture from the wine magazine, feeling like a teenage girl who was head over heels for some male rockstar. I don't get it but I have developed a real fascination for him. I am very interested in how you are doing with your investigation. Email me soon.

Love Audrey.

I decided not to email Audrey and instead decided to try something very bold. I started to type an email to John.

Dear John,

I've been recently asked to play an online game where you make up words from letters that were sent to you by another individual. It is a sort of Scrabble game. Below is a list of letters. Please form as many words as possible and email them back to me. I look forward to hearing from you.

Jade.

I hit the send button only to get an "email undeliverable" message. I checked the email address and confirmed it was correct and hit the send button again.

Then I sat in front of the screen and stared, waiting for a reply, but none was forthcoming.

Chapter 39

Back in South Africa

It really felt good to be home. All the traveling had really worn me out. James had really fallen behind in his routine paperwork at the boat brokerage business and was now working fifteen-hour days in an attempt to catch up. I never heard back from John on the Scrabble email and I was not sure what to make of it. Ruby was back in school and life in Cape Town was feeling normal. However, some of the normalcy was about to be interrupted as John walked into the office.

"Hello, Jade."

"John, this is a pleasant surprise. What brings you to Cape Town?"

"Boats and business, what else?"

"Let me call James on the cell and let him know you're here."

"Great."

"James, John Lyr is here at the office. He would like to see some boats."

"Okay, I'll be right down."

"So John, are you still interested in the Swan?"

"Yes, I hear Dr. Blink's boat is very nice."

"How did you know the Swan was owned by Dr. Blink?"

"I got the hull number from one of your office staff and then contacted the Swan International Owners group. It only took ten minutes."

"By the way, did you ever get my email I sent you about the Scrabble game?"

"Yes, I got it."

I noticed a moment of discomfort come over him.

"I don't respond to emails like that."

"Why not?"

"It's my personal philosophy."

"Okay, I can respect that."

"I am curious how the letters were selected."

"I don't know. A friend of mine who got me involved in the game forwarded those letters to me."

"That's interesting," he said in a tone that suggested he knew I was lying.

"John, who is Laura?"

His eyes shifted back and forth a few times and then the color began to fade from his face. For a moment I thought he was going to pass out, but he held on long enough for James to enter the office. James could immediately sense something was wrong.

"Hello, John. Are you okay?"

"I was just feeling a little light-headed."

"Sit down. Jade, get John some water."

I got some water from the water cooler and gave it to John. He drank it slowly.

"Thanks. I think I'm feeling better." Then he looked up at me with a very angry expression. "Never do that again, you understand me?"

"Yes, I'm sorry."

James said nothing. Then John stood up and walked outside.

"Jade, what did you say to him?"

"Nothing, really."

"Don't bullshit me!"

"Okay. I asked him who Laura was."

"Why did you do that?"

"I don't know."

James took a deep breath and walked out of the office. I watched him approach John, say a few words and then proceed down the main pier to where Dr. Blink's Swan was moored.

I could feel a real sense of shame and guilt for what I had done. I've always been quick to criticize people who ambush others and yet I knowingly and willingly ambushed John. Every person is entitled to their private life but somehow I failed to give that right to John.

Forty minutes later, John and James returned to the office. "John, I want to apologize for my question and comment. I had no right to pry."

"Apology accepted."

"So what did you think about the Swan?"

"She's very beautiful and well-maintained. It's a larger boat than I planned on buying but it may be what the doctor ordered."

I wanted to ask what doctor, but decided not to be

a wise ass.

"James, do you have a detailed specification sheet on the boat?"

"Yes. Jade, print out a full set of specifications and also email them to John's boat surveyor."

"Sure. Which surveyor should I send them to?"

"Send them to Manny Mantone; his email address is manman@sat.sa."

"I never heard of him."

"Man's been in the business a real long time. He does mostly commercial vessel surveys but I have known him awhile and trust him. He buys a lot of wine from me. His wife owns a restaurant in Franschhoek and we supply most of the wine from a variety of wine-makers."

"I didn't know you were a wine distributor."

"There's a lot you don't know about me. About the boat, expect a call from Man in the next few days. I would like him to give me an initial assessment before we talk price and terms."

"I look forward to meeting him."

"Oh, about the Laura question. I don't know any-one named Laura."

And with that said, John left the office and walked toward the parking lot. After a few seconds I walked out of the office and watched him get into his Saab Sonett.

Chapter 40

Manny

Manny Mantone or Man, as John called him, was an odd sort of fellow. He could best be described as a dark-skinned, dark-haired version of Santa Claus. His racial origin was hard to discern, but my guess was that he was a little bit of everything that had come together from centuries of inter-Caucasian breeding. Mantone, while possibly an Italian name, was more likely some version of a Middle Eastern name.

He arrived at Mac Delivery Service as scheduled.

"Good day," he said as he entered the marina office.

"Hello, how can I help you?"

"My name is Manny Mantone. I'm here to survey Head Case, the Swan that was owned by Dr. Blink."

"Who are you representing?" I asked, hoping to trip him up.

"John said you would say that. He said you are the

interrogating type."

"Really?"

"John said I should ignore all your questions."

"He said that?"

"Yep, I guess you must have quite a reputation for being nosy."

I didn't answer. "I guess you want the keys, Mr. Mantone."

"Yep, that's right."

I flipped him the keys and instructed him where to find *Head Case* and escorted him out of the office. When I returned to the office counter, I noticed that he had left his survey guide behind. I thought about chasing him down but instead decided to wait a few minutes, giving me an excuse to go down to the boat.

Five minutes later I left the marina office and started to walk down the center dock thinking about how I could crack Manny Mantone. Just as I was about to step onto *Head Case*, Manny stuck his head out of the companionway.

"Oh, I see you have my surveying guide."

"Yes."

"Thanks for bringing it down to me."

"You're welcome. So what do you think of her?"

"She's a beautiful vessel."

"Yes, she certainly is. The former owner really took good care of her."

"John told me the vessel is being held by the estate of Dr. Blink."

"Yes, that's right."

"What happened to the good doctor?"

"He died in a fire."

Manny cocked his head. I could tell I struck a nerve.

"A fire?"

"Yes. I think he may have been in Moscow when he died."

Manny twitched. He was showing signs that I was onto something.

"Look, I like to do my surveying alone so maybe you can go back to the office."

"Sure thing."

I noticed beads of sweat forming on his forehead, indicating he was uncomfortable with the conversation. "Okay," I thought to myself, "one more fact confirmed."

An hour later James came into the office. "I thought John had said this Manny fellow was doing a cursory review of *Head Case*. I was just down there and he's going over the boat with a fine-tooth comb. Given what I saw, I feel pretty certain John is going to buy the boat so long as the survey goes well."

"You think that maybe Manny is looking for something that may be hidden on the boat?"

"What do you mean?"

"I don't know. Maybe it's my conspiracy theory paranoia talking."

"Jade, life is not a conspiracy."

"You're probably right."

Four hours later, Manny Mantone still had not completed the survey. James had run a few errands so I decided to walk down to *Head Case*. Manny was sitting in the cockpit filling out the survey report.

"So Mr. Mantone, what do you think?"

"She's a real fine vessel, all right. If I had the money I would buy her myself."

"How much longer will you be? We close the office in about half an hour."

"I should be done by then."

"Okay, just drop the keys off before you leave."

"Will do."

Half an hour later, Manny walked into the office.

"Here are the keys."

"Thanks."

"Do you mind if I use the wash room?"

"Go ahead, it's just behind me."

Seconds later, I could hear the sound of Manny's urine stream hitting the water in the toilet but that was not all I heard. I felt a temporary dizziness come over me and I tried to figure out what was happening. Manny flushed the toilet and returned to the counter.

"I noticed you were humming something while you were in the bathroom."

"Yep, my ex-wife always hummed that little tune. Do you know it?"

"I think so."

"Yep, it's sad what happened to her."

"What's that?"

"We were married for about ten years. She started to have some issues with her eyes and eventually became blind. One day she vanished and I never saw her again. From time to time people said they saw her wandering through the bush but after years of trying to find her, I finally gave up. The courts granted me a divorce."

He reached into his wallet and pulled out an old

tattered picture. It was a picture of a beautiful woman. "That's her twenty-five years ago."

"Wow, she's beautiful."

"Yep, she sure was. Well, that's the past and this is the present."

I said nothing, but was almost sure it was La Teek.

"Oh, by the way, I found this lying behind one of the cushions on Dr. Blink's boat. I think it belongs to you."

Manny extended his hand. I was speechless for a second.

"Thanks, Mr. Mantone."

As Manny left the office, I opened up the envelope addressed to Jade Morison. Inside was a small leather pouch full of letters. I sorted them and confirmed that they matched the letters in the pouch that was given to me by La Teek. Now I started to wonder: Did La Teek give the pouch to Dr. Blink or did Dr. Blink give the pouch to La Teek? It would be a question that was never answered.

Chapter 41

The Last 45 Days

Unlike certain things that happen in the blink of an eye, other things happen at their own pace. Over the last forty-five days a series of important events either came to light and were resolved, or in the case of other events, finally got resolved after a long period of time.

Not long after Manny's survey, John Lyr purchased *Head Case*. He didn't negotiate the price but did negotiate the terms. In the end we netted a commission of $45,000 U.S. though we did have to concede on providing him one year's free slip usage. I had also recommended Manny to other clients and while this caused him to be around Mac Delivery Service more often, I never ventured back into any discussion about John or LaTeek and that's because I didn't need to.

I had made extensive plans around Audrey and Su's planned trip to South Africa, which included a trip to

John's home and a tour of M.S. Vineyards. I had several conversations with John about our initial meeting in the airport and during the conversations, he admitted that he had started staring at Ruby because of her strange eyes. He told me that he had never before seen a person with eyes like hers, where one eye was light blue and the other was deep brown, but I knew he was lying. John had also stopped wearing his wedding band. I guessed it was either because it raised too many questions or that whatever the ring had represented no longer held the significance to him as it had in the past.

As for Ruby, kids at her school had started teasing her about her odd look and James and I had started to have conversations about whether she should conceal her oddity with a single brown or blue contact lens. On the financial front, Mac Delivery Service continued to do well and our college fund for Ruby was starting to be fully funded.

Audrey and I had talked to each other weekly and I was convinced that her excitement about their trip was more about meeting John than it was about us, and I was comfortable with that. James Bond and my James had seen each other a few times when Mr. Bond was in Cape Town to look after the construction of his new boat and James and I were having some discussions about assisting Mr. Bond with the delivery of the boat to Annapolis, Maryland. Regarding other information on John, Mr. Bond had very little new info that was helpful.

Mickey Dermott's emails had trickled to a glacial pace, though he did manage to get some additional information on the money John spent in Moscow at the private hospital. The information only confirmed what I had already suspected.

One of the more fruitful changes in my life was the pattern of my sleep and the quality of my dreams. Each night I would not drift off to sleep, but rather crash into sleep. My dreaming was superb. Each night small bits of information were revealed to me and little by little, the solution to the puzzle became apparent. I now understood everything that I had read in Dr. Blink's journal. But more importantly, I had a better understanding of Michael's journals as well, and what it must have been like to live in his twisted world. I understood the messages from Jodii and the comments Michael made to me during Ruby's hypnosis sessions.

I was able to get some additional information about John from having filed his ownership papers as I transferred *Head Case* from the estate of Dr. Blink to M.S. Vineyards. However, the one thing that continued to stump all of us was how to correctly arrange the tiles given to me by La Teek and her husband, so they would spell words. There were only two people who could do that and neither John nor Manny was willing to reveal the secret of the tiles.

The week before Audrey was scheduled to depart Hampton for the long trip to South Africa, she called me with a suggestion on how to find the meaning of the tiles. I picked up the phone.

"Hello Jade, how are you?"

"Very well. How are things with you?"

"Winter is arriving early here and I think we should stop talking about global warming and start talking about global freezing. I'll be very happy to get to the Southern Hemisphere."

"I agree; our winter was really tough as well."

"I want to let you know that last night I found a new application on the Internet that may be of value to us. This application called Jumble-Jumble takes random letters and makes legitimate words out of them."

"Audrey, we have tried this before."

"I know, but this appears to be more expansive. I ran the letters and got 300 hits. Many were foreign words and simple words which we've all seen before but some were very interesting and worth further analysis. It did some searches on the new words and found some real interesting facts. I'll send you the list of them later today and you can ponder them. There are probably 10 of them you should pay attention to."

"Well, maybe we'll have a breakthrough."

"Maybe so. At any rate, look them over and we can talk about it when I arrive."

"Sure thing. Travel safely."

"Thanks, I'll see you at the airport."

"I can't wait."

Chapter 42

Love at First Sight

To be honest, I can't remember if I was struck with love at first sight or not. James and I never really talked about it. Our love for each other just happened in St. Barts fourteen years ago and while I can remember that day as if it were yesterday, I don't really remember the first time I saw him or what I felt. I guess I believe in love at first sight. Why not? After all, I did witness it on December 24, Christmas Eve.

Audrey and Su's arrival at Cape Town airport was delayed due to a variety of issues. They had flown from Newport News to JFK in New York and then boarded South African Airlines with a direct flight to Johannesburg. Johannesburg Airport had always been the most screwed up airport in the world, with the highest luggage theft rate and highest hassle rate of any other airport. All that could have gone wrong went wrong and while the South African Airlines flight landed on time, it took two hours before Audrey and Su had collected their bags, dealt with immigration, cleared customs and rechecked their bags to Cape Town.

I had encouraged them to fly direct to Cape Town but due to a series of logistical issues they had to fly to Johannesburg first. Ruby had accompanied me to the Cape Town airport and was very anxious to see Su and Audrey. Our reunion was wonderful, though I must say that both Audrey and Su looked like they had been taken to hell and back again.

"Jade, great to be here," Audrey said in between her yawns.

"It's great to have you here in South Africa. How was the flight?"

"The flight was not bad though really, really long. Su slept most of the way but I hardly slept at all."

"Why, too much on your mind?"

"Well, I would have been fine if you didn't tell me we were going to John's home on Christmas Eve."

"You're right; I probably should not have told you until you got here."

"By the way, why do you suppose he invited us?"

"I don't know. I guess he is just trying to be friendly and besides, he and James have become pretty chummy lately."

"Very interesting."

"Yeah. It's a guy-boat thing."

The ride back to Cape Town was strange. Audrey and I said very little to each other, primarily because it was hard to talk over Su and Ruby's conversation and besides, Audrey and I liked eaves-dropping in on their conversation. They both had little to say about John but a few comments were made that made me realize that Audrey and Su had been having a lot of discussion about him.

Nothing very eventful happened between their arrival in Cape Town and Christmas Eve. I spent most of the time showing them around the area, spent some time at the marina, and made a trip to Scarborough, where we walked on the beach.

James's previous infatuation with Audrey seemed to have lessened which I truly appreciated. Christmas Eve was now upon us and Audrey's nervousness was very apparent. Audrey emerged from the guest room looking as beautiful as one could imagine. I could see James's breath being taken away as he gazed at her. I thought back to Michael's journal and felt so sad that he had such a short time with Audrey before he died.

As the five of us walked to the car, James's cell phone rang.

"James, let it roll to voicemail."

"I can't; I'm on call tonight."

The call went on for a few minutes and I could tell that there was a problem at the marina.

"What's going on?" I asked.

"There's a problem with one of the boats."

"Which boat?"

"Stuart Mark's sloop."

"What's the problem?"

"It's sinking. I have to go down there. Tell John I

apologize."

"Okay, call me on the cell phone and let me know how things are going."

"Okay. I'll give you a call."

The sixty-mile drive to Franschhoek took about ninety minutes. We were given an address that put John's house very close to M.S. Vineyards. As we turned in to the gravel driveway, I was taken by the size and the beauty of his house. This was not a single guy's home. I could sense a real feminine touch to the gardens that surrounded the property. I pulled up and parked the car next to John's Saab Sonett. Audrey looked very uncomfortable.

"Boy, this is weird. It's like I'm going to visit Michael."

I said nothing but in the back of my mind I was thinking, "Good guess."

Ruby and Su had also grown quiet. Su took a hard look at the Saab. "Mom, it's like Daddy's car."

"Yes, I know."

The walk from the car to the front door took what seemed like a very long time but in truth, it was only about fifty feet. The knocker on the front door was in the figure of a large "S" and I wondered if it might have been from the previous owner or somehow linked to John's past. I could hear John's footsteps behind the door. Then the deadbolt retracted and John opened the door. Audrey stood to the side of the door, so the first two people he saw were Ruby and me.

"Jade, Ruby, Merry Christmas."

John leaned forward toward Ruby and gave her a

hug.

"And who is this?"

"I'm Su Kenney."

Then John looked up and found himself face to face with Audrey.

"It's you," John said.

"Excuse me," said Audrey. But John said nothing, not really knowing what to say.

"Have we met before?" John said, obviously searching for a way to get out of his previous comment.

"No, not really, but I did see a picture of you in a wine magazine."

John reached into his pocket and pulled out a handkerchief, which he used to wipe his brow.

"Well, come in. Let me get you a glass of wine. Come into the living room and make yourselves comfortable."

As John walked away, Audrey looked at me and whispered, "He is so handsome."

I just smiled. The four of us walked into the living room. The living room was set up with two sofas facing each other. In between them was a large coffee table that had some light hors d'oeuvres placed on a plate that sat on a white doily. The doily, once again, was not a guy thing.

Audrey, Su and Ruby sat down and started to engage in small talk, while I walked into the kitchen where John was standing. He was frozen, not moving an inch and not tending to the wine for his guests.

"John, are you okay?"

He turned his head toward me. "What did you say?"

"I said, are you okay?"

"Your friend, Audrey?"

"Yes, what about her?"

"I know her, I've seen her before."

"John, that is very unlikely."

He wiped his brow again. Then he pulled out a bottle of red wine and began to decant it.

"She's just as I imagined her."

I could tell he was talking to himself and had forgotten I was standing there. I said nothing. Then he looked at me and regained his awareness.

"What would the girls like to drink?"

"Anything will be fine."

"Would lemonade be okay?"

"Sure, they'll love that."

John walked back to the living room. I walked behind him. Both he and Audrey were clearly uncomfortable because I think they wanted to be alone but didn't know how to get rid of the girls and me. John poured the wine with one eye on the glass and one eye on Audrey. He raised his glass and toasted.

"Here's to happiness now and forever."

We all went to click glasses but the only glass John was interested in was Audrey's. Ruby and Su giggled because they could see that John was so taken with Audrey.

I broke in, "John, would it be okay if I took the girls over to the vineyard across the street?"

"Sure, please do."

"Okay. We'll be back in fifteen minutes. Come on, girls."

Ruby and Su walked out the door. As we walked

across the street, I could only imagine what was happening with John and Audrey, but I already knew.

"Jade, what do you think is going on?" Su asked.

"They are just getting to know each other."

"They are probably kissing," Ruby said.

Su giggled again. We walked to the fields trying to kill time, but due to biological needs of Ruby's, we were forced to return. Once again we knocked on the door. This time Audrey came to the door. The girls walked in and Audrey walked out.

"Oh my god, Jade, I think I'm in love."

"I'm not surprised."

We walked back in. Ruby and Su had found the bathroom and had returned to their spot on the sofa. John and Audrey sat together on the other couch. I decided to sit with the girls. John had placed several gift bags near the coffee table. He reached in and gave each girl a gift.

"Go ahead and open them."

The girls started to open the gifts. Under the wrapping paper was a cardboard box and inside the cardboard box was a beautiful music box. The girls were surprised, but I was not. Ruby wound the mechanism and then opened the box. The music was very familiar to Ruby and me. Then he handed Audrey and me decorative wooden boxes. Inside each box was a bottle of wine.

"Thank you, John. This is very nice," I said.

"These bottles are what's left of the best wine we have ever produced. They won three wine tastings, two in Europe and one in South Africa."

I studied the label for a few seconds and then returned it to the wooden box. Then I took a deep breath. "Okay John, now it's time for your Christmas gift."

Chapter 43

The Gift

John sat there, waiting for us to hand him a gift, but there was no physical gift to give. Audrey moved toward John and took his hand.

Audrey started, "John, please be open to what Jade has to say."

John looked confused. "What do you mean?"

I took a deep breath and began. "John, I know virtually everything there is to know about us and I mean the five of us. Have you ever dreamed about a black slave girl?"

He said nothing.

"The slave girl's name is Angel Lehcar. She murdered the slave foreman who killed her brother and father and raped her and her mother. She was hung for her deed. Did you get a good look at her eyes?"

John remained silent.

"Did you ever dream about a boy and his sister? They were immigrants from Sweden. He died in a car accident before midlife. Did you get a good look at his eyes?"

Now his discomfort was growing as he kept shifting his eyes toward Ruby.

"John, did you ever dream about a man who also died rather young and who had an obsession with staring at ceiling fans? And oh, by the way, he owned a Saab Sonett, and was also an avid sailor."

John was now in shock and still silent.

I continued on. "Five years ago while traveling in Moscow you were involved in a terrible car accident with your family."

Now he was visibly shaking and tears started to roll down his cheeks.

"Your wife, Laura, and daughters Yanna and Rose were killed, but you survived. Your pain was so horrible that you changed your identity to John Lyr. I also know that Lyr stands for the names of your wife and daughters."

"Okay, please stop," John said.

"John, let her go on," pleaded Audrey.

"John, there is a reason for this. My guess is that all these dreams of all these people probably started shortly after you lost your family. I also believe that you have had dreams of Ruby, Audrey, and Su."

John started nodding his head.

"John, it's okay. I need to explain why this has happened to you."

"Wait Jade, please stop."

John got up and left the room.

"Jade, maybe we should stop," said Audrey.

"Trust me, we are doing the right thing."

We sat in silence until John returned.

"Follow me. I think you should see something."

We walked down a long hallway and into a room that was a private study. On the wall were a series of drawings.

"I drew these about two years ago."

The first drawing was Angel Lehcar. The pencil drawing showed her with one light gray eye and one black eye. She was a pretty girl but one whose life had been beaten out of her.

"This is the Swedish boy you mentioned."

He was standing next to a sailboat. He also had the blue eye, brown eye oddity.

Then there was a picture of Michael.

"This is your fan guy."

Audrey and Su began crying.

I interrupted him. "That fan guy was Audrey's husband and Su's father."

"Oh my god, I'm so sorry."

John walked over to Audrey and Su and hugged them.

Then he opened up the desk drawer and pulled out a folder.

"I painted these last year."

There was a picture of Ruby and Audrey.

"Jade, can you explain what the hell has happened to me?"

"Yes, but first I need to know the answer to the tiles. What are the tiles supposed to spell? Tell me, John, and I can explain the rest."

John reached into his pocket and pulled out one of his business cards and gave it to me.

"So, what's this?"

"Turn it over."

On the back of the card were the words Manakin Sabot.

"What is Manakin Sabot?"

Then he opened the middle drawer and pulled out four canceled passports. He handed three of them to me. They were all Canadian issued passports. The name on the first passport was Laura Sabot. The second read Yanna Sabot and the third, Rose Sabot. Then he handed me the fourth passport. I opened it up. The name Manakin Sabot appeared on the face page. The picture on the passport was of John.

"So you are Man."

"Yes, that's who I used to be before the accident. Man died that day along with Laura, Yanna and Rose. So with a little help from the Canadian government, Manakin Sabot vanished and John Lyr was born."

There was a long period of silence as we all tried to absorb the tragedy that had struck John and his family.

"Jade, simply tell me why all this has happened." We walked back to the living room and sat down. Once again, Audrey and John sat together.

"It's all about your soul. Souls are reused. Think of it as reincarnation. Angel's soul was passed to Jost, who passed it on to Michael Kenney, Audrey's late husband and Su's father. Michael's soul was passed on to Ruby. But souls are also shared and somehow you share a soul or at least some part of it with Michael Kenney."

"Jade, while this sounds so unreal, the evidence is

overwhelming."

"Souls reach out to each other. I see that with Michael and Ruby and now with you. I knew all along that someday Michael would lead me to his shared soul. This was a way to solve the pain of two people and to enrich two others. Somewhere you were touched by a woman named La Teek, Manny Mantone's wife. The music boxes you gave the girls originally belonged to Yanna and Rose. You bought them from La Teek. They play the same song Ruby sings. La Teek gave me the tiles."

"How can that be? La Teek died years ago."

"No, she did not. She is very much alive."

By now, we were all emotionally exhausted. Our heads were spinning and everybody was in tears. John was the first to break the silence.

"There are two more things. One is something I have to say and the other is something I have to do. First I want to thank you for bringing some sanity to my insane life. There have been so many things that have been haunting me and now I know why and for what purpose. Now the thing I must do."

John placed his thumb and index finger around his eye and removed a brown contact lens, revealing his blue eye.

"I guess I don't need this anymore."

I looked toward Ruby and realized that she had left the room. A look of concern came across Audrey's, John's and Su's faces.

"Stay here." I walked quietly down the hallway expecting to find Ruby back in the study. I could feel footsteps behind me and knew the others were following close behind. We approached the study. The door was opened halfway. We peered in. Ruby sat on the floor opposite the picture of Michael. There appeared to be a glow around her. Her body shimmered as if it were translucent. She raised her hands toward the picture. I couldn't tell if her eyes were opened but I wanted to believe that they were. I could hear a faint whisper emanating from the picture.

"Ruby?"

"Yes, it's me."

"You have called me once again."

"I'm afraid, Michael."

"Why?"

"I think this may be the end."

"Yes, we are very close."

"Does that mean I won't be able to talk to you anymore?"

"I think so, but I don't know for sure. Ruby, I'm tired and our work is done."

"No, it can never be done."

"Ruby, don't waste any more of your time or any more of your dreams on me. You have cured my broken soul. It's time for me to go and to join the others. That is my place. You have your families now. You have your sister. You have my daughter. That is your place."

Then the conversation ended and the glow that surrounded Ruby faded away. We all stood there numb and confused. Ruby stood up and turned around. She was not startled by our presence. She knew we were watching. Then she walked over to the picture of Michael Kenney. She raised her hands and touched the edge of the frame. Then she turned around.

"I'm really going to miss him."
"We all will," I replied.

Epilogue

One year later and after long negotiations with the Canadian and U.S. passport authorities, and with a little help from Mickey Dermott, Audrey Kenney and Manakin Sabot were wed. At the wedding ceremony, Man and Audrey stood at the altar with Su and Ruby, who held their wedding rings. Audrey had decided to take a new name, Audrey Kenney Sabot, and it occurred to me in a strange way that Audrey got her husband back, Su got her father back and Man got his wife and two daughters back.

Shortly after the wedding, the Kenneys' home in Hampton was rented to Mickey Dermott, who had left his assignment in Paris and moved back to Hampton.

Audrey and Man purchased a house within walking distance of our home, so Ruby and Su could be together.

As for James and me, life has been good, very good. Ruby will join James in the delivery room so we can all meet the newest addition to the Morison family. The doctor said the ultrasound indicates a baby boy, who we will name Michael Kenney Morison.

As for Michael Kenney, I believe he has found peace, and all of his issues—whatever they were—seem to have been resolved, as none of us has heard from him for some time.

Post Script

Now She Haunts Me

I passed this child along the road,
Her stare said "Help me,"
But I did nothing,
And now she haunts me.

Her dirty face, her sunken eyes,
Her mouth said "Feed me,"
But I did nothing,
And now she haunts me.

She rubbed her hands and shivered gently,
She said, "Please warm me,"
But I did nothing,
And now she haunts me.

Her voice was broken, she spoke so softly,
She said "Please teach me,"
But I did nothing,
And now she haunts me.

This man walked passed me along the road,
I felt so desperate, I hoped he'd help me,
But he did nothing,
So I will haunt him.

Kenneth Krakaur

35

I've got that look now,
The one I've seen before,
In faces that have seen everything,
And know there's no more.

They laughed every laugh,
Cried every tear,
Felt every feeling,
And feared every fear.

I know that look now,
I've seen it before,
On the face of a woman,
A girl just before.

Joaquin 1986

Fear

The ocean I like,
But not in the middle,
Where my security loses its store.
Where some find glory,
I find fear,
I'd rather be by the shore.

Joaquin

A note from the author:

On the Edge of My Shadow is the third book in The Reincarnations of Michael Kenney Trilogy. I have tried to weave together both familiar and new characters as I continued the saga into the next generation. The three books comprising the trilogy explore the timeless questions of death, rebirth, love, and the persistence of our soul.

Beyond the Shore
Book One of the Reincarnations of Michael Kenney Trilogy

"Wanted: Experienced cook to join delivery crew. Sailing in 30 days (Cape Town to the Caribbean). Contact John at Mac Delivery Service, Cape Town."

And so begins a journey of discovery. Filled with rich detail about sailing, sailboats, and the people who make their lives crewing, *Beyond the Shore* is also about a spiritual journey: one that finds heart and meaning in the wisdom traditions of Judaism and Buddhism.

Beginning in South Africa with a help wanted ad and a chance encounter with a modern mystic, twenty-one year old Jade sets out to discover herself and her place in a world from which she feels oddly disconnected. Her physical journey takes her from Cape Town to Brazil to the Caribbean to the Chesapeake Bay, but her real journey is an internal quest for a way of being in relationship to the world. Anchored by the thirteen principles of the Bujew and guided by a tiny packet of sand from a Tibetan Buddhist mandala, Jade finds her own heart *Beyond the Shore.*

In The Blink of An Eye

Book Two of the Reincarnations of Michael Kenney Trilogy

While the past is the most tangible element of time; It is the future that ranks second as we tend to shape the future around our knowledge of the past."

Thousands of times a day we blink, and with each blink, there is a sliver of darkness that is created as the eyelid passes over the pupil. Most people don't see the sliver or choose to ignore what exists in the darkness. This is not the case for Michael Kenney.

Obsessed with analyzing the images he sees in the darkness, Michael sets out on a quest to understand his past and his future. He discovers his pre-incarnations and the people he once was. But that is not enough. His need to understand what lies beyond death takes him on a physical and spiritual journey.

His physical journey takes him to the Caribbean and South Africa while his spiritual journey takes him deep into the teachings of Buddhism and Judaism. Anchored by the wisdom and compassion traditions of his beliefs, Michael Kenney learns that what lies beyond death is found *In the Blink of an Eye.*

Beyond The Shore, published in 2007, and *In the Blink of An Eye* published in 2009 are both available at www.bujewpress.com or at www.amazon.com.

Made in the USA
Columbia, SC
20 April 2025

56828331R00141